WHAT DO
MONSTERS
FEAR?

WHAT DO
MONSTERS
FEAR?

MATT HAYWARD

POST MORTEM PRESS
CINCINNATI

For Anna Muhlbach

PROLOGUE

June 22ⁿᵈ, 1978

Heather stepped into Harris Dawson's private practice and whistled, her neck craned to get a better view of the overhead chandelier. "I've never seen one of those in real life," she said. "Only in the movies. It's gorgeous. The couch, real leather?"

Harris Dawson closed the office door and stood by the fireplace. He smiled. "I appreciate your kind words, Heather, but if it's all right with you, I'd like to talk about your late husband."

Heather's face fell. She eased herself onto the couch and stared at the rug; a Russian antique Harris had acquired the previous week. "Yes. We can talk about him. You're just so *young*, I didn't expect such a nice place, that's all."

"Quite all right." Harris picked a notebook from the table and skimmed the first page. "With the office in town being fumigated, I didn't want to miss an opportunity to talk to you. You sure you don't mind being here?"

"Where else would I have to go?"

Harris gave a tight smile. "Living on the streets must be trying. You say it's been one week?"

"Eight days now." She sighed. "After Eddie passed, I just . . . lost myself. You have no idea how much it means to me that you'd offer me your services for free. I wish I could repay you, Harris. With everywhere I could've been, winding up sleeping in the alleyway of a shrink wasn't in the cards. I mean, what were the chances?"

"Slim," Harris said. If Heather noticed that his notebook contained doodles of smiley faces instead of text, she gave no indication. "This is my pleasure to have you here. I don't do this for the money. I do this to help people. Your family, you told me they're . . . ."

"Out of the picture, yes. Eddie's family took me in as one of their own but I lost contact and haven't been brave enough to call. Maybe, with your help, I will?"

"Perhaps." Harris finished scribbling an elongated penis onto a matchstick man and placed the notebook aside. "I'd like to talk about what happened to Eddie. What comes to mind?"

At the sound of her husband's name, Heather winced. She tucked a lock of unwashed hair behind her ear. "Just a heart attack. No one to blame. No life insurance. Just . . . That's it. Only forty-three, can you believe it? The garage didn't offer anything besides condolences."

"And you fear life without him?"

"Every minute of it."

"And, Heather, what if I told you that you could see him again?"

Harris fought to keep the laughter down as the woman's eyes widened. Her mouth fell open and she clutched the couch, her knuckles white. "That's not funny, Doctor Dawson, not funny at all!"

"No, I quite agree. But only because it's not a joke."

Heather hoisted herself from the couch, her nostrils flaring. "I knew it. I knew you were too good to be true. Oh poor homeless Heather, who would actually want to help *you*, right? Well, I'll show you, Dawson. I don't need you, or anybody."

The door handle jittered. Harris placed his hands behind his back and watched as his stomach cartwheeled and his heart jackhammered.

"Who is that?" Heather asked, moving behind the couch as if for protection. "What's going on here?"

"I told you it wasn't a joke, dear. I have somebody I'd like you to meet."

The door creaked open. A rancid, shriveled hand quivered as it slipped around the polished mahogany frame. Then Eddie entered the room.

Heather screamed, her knees locking together. Her eyes bulged from their sockets and her hands squeezed into tight fists. Eddie plodded forward, his alabaster skin catching the glare of the overhead chandelier. Dirt and decay wafted from him in thick, nauseous waves. Harris pinched his nose, chuckling.

"That's not my husband!" Heather roared, jerking left and

right like a cornered animal. "*That's not my husband!*"

Then Eddie clutched her throat.

As Heather gagged and smacked at the deadman's hands, Harris returned to doodling, trying his best to ignore the violent struggle. He had almost finished an elephant wearing roller skates when Heather finally gave her last breath and fell still. Sighing, Harris snapped his notebook closed and crossed the room.

He grimaced at the deep red finger marks on the woman's neck. "Strangulation? Are you sure that was the smartest move? Impeccable conditions are required, my Lord, and finding another is out of the question, I—"

The deadman growled, his eyes wide. Dawson's stomach lurched.

"I'm sorry," he said. "I won't question you again."

The deadman eased himself down beside his wife's corpse, lying like lovers sleeping the long sleep. His eyes closed.

Dawson's hair prickled as a gust of air blew by, carrying with it the brown stench of rotting flesh and forcing the taste of copper to his tongue. His ears popped, the pressure of the room changing. He kept his eyes on the dead woman, knowing that at any moment, she would move. Once that happened, Harris would make the phone call to his superiors and enjoy the champagne he'd put on ice earlier that day. One last night of relaxation before Hell came to Earth.

Heather's body jittered, her legs banging the hardwood. Her eyes trembled as if full of scurrying ants. The scene reminded Harris of a victim in the throes of a vicious epileptic fit.

Yes, Dawson thought, *that's it . . . Easy does it, Phobos . . . Easy does it . . .*

Then her stomach began to bulge. Harris gripped the couch in a panic. "No! No! Easy! I can't do this again, *I can't find you another!*"

But the dead lady's stomach continued swelling. With a crack, a bone jutted from her forearm, sending a spray of blood across the Russian rug. Her face puffed out, pushing her eyes to either side of her head like some kind of grotesque kid's toy.

Then her stomach exploded.

Harris flinched as warm, wet slabs slapped him. He recoiled in disgust, trying to wipe his face clean but only managing to smear the goop. He slipped on something that felt like a slug and clutched the wall for support, catching himself just before tumbling. Panting, he eyed the room.

Crimson splats stained the walls. His prized collection of vintage hardbacks dripped in gore, suffering the worst of the blast. A metallic smell mingled with the rotten now, making him gag and cough. Overhead, the chandelier swung, throwing dancing shadows this way and that.

The dead woman's carcass sat open on the floor, disfigured beyond all recognition, and anger boiled inside Harris Dawson.

"I needed *results!*" he shouted, slamming a polished shoe down into a puddle of something nasty. "What am I supposed to tell them now? They'll have me killed for wasting their time!"

Easy, he warned himself, knowing Phobos still lurked somewhere in the room. He felt the presence. *Piss him off and he'll take you instead . . .*

Harris rubbed his forehead. "Okay," he said. "I'll make the call and request more time. With any hope, they'll give me another chance but who knows . . . Fuck . . . Now I've got to take care of this mess. You need patience, my Lord. Patience. It might be a while before I can get something new together, but I'll do it . . . Next time will be different." Harris withdrew a handkerchief from his jacket pocket and dabbed his face. "I'll find a way," he said. "I always do."

CHAPTER ONE

January 28th, 2017

Peter dropped the razor blade into the bathroom sink. His hands shook. In the fogged-up mirror, he caught sight of his reflection.

"How'd you let it get so bad, Pete?"

He wiped his eyes on his shirtsleeve and took a deep breath, easing his spasming chest. He couldn't stop crying. Earlier, this decision had been a sterile, emotionless one, as simple as deciding on what to eat for supper. A matter-of-fact choice. Peter was going to kill himself. But now, he felt different.

"Stop looking at the damn blade, man."

He'd woken with the idea that morning, and after showering, eating breakfast, and getting dressed, he'd taken a walk to the drugstore, where he'd purchased a pack of disposable razors and a newspaper. The store clerk told him to have a good day, a smile on his face. Peter said that he would.

Now, that same newspaper sat propped behind the taps, leaning against the mirror. He'd left it there to show the date, just in case some days passed before anyone found the body. Nobody called his apartment, not anymore. Not since he'd become a such a burden.

Peter closed his eyes, the sight of the razor blade making him nauseous.

The whole experience had been like watching some actor in a depressing movie, his eyes the screen. Smashing the cheap plastic of the razor hadn't fazed him, but putting the cold steel to his flesh had, causing realization to break through like a radio station from white noise. That'd stopped him. That, and what he'd seen in the mirror besides himself.

"You can't leave Bethany to deal with this alone. Get a grip." His voice sounded thick and watery as it bounced off the dirty, tiled walls. Pushing himself from the sink, Peter cried out and crammed his palms into his eyes. "I'll give it one more shot..."

Drying his nose on his sleeve, he snatched the paper from the sink and stepped into the apartment's living room. Not *his* living room, as his grandmother liked to call it: *the apartment's* living room. He'd never admit this small, single-bedroomed flat was all he had now that his music days were over.

Falling onto the couch, Peter ran a hand through his greasy hair and sighed as moisture seeped into the butt of his jeans from a spilled beer. In his hands, the reason he'd stopped himself, besides Bethany, glared back. An advertisement in the back of the paper. One for a clinic.

DAWSON REHABILITATION
DRUG-FREE RESIDENTIAL REHAB
DON'T BE AFRAID TO REACH OUT

Admitting you need help is difficult, but taking that first step starts here.

At Dawson Rehabilitation, we boast a team of non-judgmental professionals in a clean and confidential environment to help you on your road to recovery.

Join our two-week detox course

DON'T BE AFRAID TO CALL
REMEMBER: WE ARE HERE TO HELP

The advert, in its baby-blue box, gave a free-of-charge phone number. Reading it over and over, Peter sniffled. He'd never seen a rehabilitation center advertise before. Did they usually do that? He didn't think so.

Say it, Peter. Admit it. You're a goddamn alcoholic.

Peter spoke to the empty room. "I . . . I need help."

There. Doesn't that feel better? Your friends got married, soared in their careers, and distanced themselves because they could actually control *their habits. A couple of beers on the weekend, maybe a bump of charlie in the bathroom, no big deal, right? Not to them. But to you? Jesus H. Christ . . . And they knew you were on a slippery path, too, you know. They were just too kind to say it to you. And isn't that the worst part of all this? That they think of you like the old family pet they once knew and loved, now waiting to take its last, shaking breath? And when it happens they'll secretly be relieved. Because the Peter they knew showed so much promise in his youth. So much determination.*

And somehow . . . Somewhere along the way it just . . . Slipped.

You're a loser.

"It's not true . . ."

Nobody wants to be around you because it's sad. It's pathetic. You work in a coffee shop and dream of being a professional musician again. And maybe, just maybe, you had a chance once, but you just couldn't ever put in the hours and work hard. You always half-assed. Always.

There. Doesn't that feel better to admit? Sure, when you were eighteen you got signed to a record label. And yes, they gave you money, and wasn't that nice? Your friends were proud, your peers were jealous. You toured the country on something you built from scratch when everyone else said that you couldn't. Your grandmother was so proud, Peter. Beth *was proud.*

But Pete, the band broke up three years ago, remember? And those royalty checks are getting smaller and smaller and smaller . . . And what have you done since but pity yourself? Not a goddamn thing, that's what. Oh, except leave Bethany up shit-creek without a paddle, of course. So here's the ultimatum, kid: Get help or leave a mess. But make a fucking choice, all right?

Swiping his cell phone from the couch, Peter composed himself. He flicked through his contacts until he found the one that he wanted.

The phone rang. Once. Twice.

"Hello? Grandma?"

"Peter, hello. What's the matter?"

Peter laughed despite the situation. The old woman could read his goddamn mind.

"Is everything all right?"

Peter's smile faded. "Um, no, actually."

If you must know, I was just getting ready to off myself!

Stop it. Get yourself together, man.

"Petey? What's the matter?"

With a deep breath, Peter forced the truth out like vomit. "I'm in trouble, Grandma. I need a little help . . ." Then tears started again, hot and fast. "I need to talk. Do you mind if I come by?"

"Of course not, Peter." The old woman sounded close to crying herself. "Come over, please. Come, come."

"Okay."

Peter ended the call and blinked to clear his eyes. His nerves were shot. Pushing himself from the couch, he worked his hands in and out of fists, his palms slick with sweat.

"Time to face the music," he said. ". . . If I can."

The apartment's stale odor turned his stomach. He hadn't eaten since breakfast. Dishes jutted from the sink, undone and filthy, and the sight only made him feel worse.

"When I get back, this place is getting cleaned up and Beth'll like it. So will the . . ."

Don't think about that right now, Pete. One step at a time. Get a move on.

The wind spat thick droplets of rain at the window as Peter crossed to it and peered outside. Through the grimy glass, he watched fat, dark clouds cast the day in constant gloom. Shaking his head, he went to the couch and scooped his raincoat, an old synthetic one with a hood. Slipping into the coat, his stomach fluttered with adrenaline.

"Oh, please don't . . . Not now . . ."

He darted for the sink, making it just in time. A stream of warmth shot up his throat, splashing the dishes and leaving him gasping for breath. He clutched the counter, forcing himself to relax. "That's definitely breakfast, at least."

His stomach gave another shudder at the idea of telling his grandmother *everything* but he quickly steadied himself, his muscles loosening. He needed to tell her. Not only for himself, but for Bethany, too—if he ever wanted to make a life with her. His grandmother needed to know . . .

"Because she has money," Peter said, turning the tap to rinse out the sink. "And treatment ain't cheap. This is real bottom-feeder shit."

As the water ran down the drain, taking chunks of half-digested cereal off the plates and bowls, Peter leaned in and took a sip. He gargled before spitting, the burning sensation in the back of his throat soothed. With the plates sick-free, he shut off the tap before swiping his keys from the tabletop, his mind reeling.

You're really going to ask poor ol' Grandma for money?

"She'd want me to, if she knew . . ."

And will you have enough self-control to stop yourself from going and buying a truckload of booze to comatose yourself for a year with that cash? Really?

Peter stood at the door, the keys dangling from his hand. The razor blade called from the sink again.

"She'd want me to ask for help . . . And I do need it. I *really* do. She'd want to be there for me."

A harsh, no-bullshit voice spoke up: *Exactly. She's always there for you. That's why you never took a chance and worked hard after music, because she's your safety net. She'd always come running whenever you called, and you knew she would. Jesus Christ, look . . . Just kill yourself, all right? This is sad, sad stuff, man.*

The idea hit like a punch to the gut and Peter's legs trembled.

"No . . . No, I can do this. I'm not afraid to ask for help."

The tough, no-bullshit voice didn't reply.

Peter dabbed at his face to clear it before opening the door. In the hallway, cold, damp air prickled his skin. He closed the door and shivered. The steps leading to the first floor were wet from other's boots and shoes and he held the railing tight. The wall to his left boasted a faded green paint, dirty from years of built-up crud. *Jesus,* he thought. *No wonder I was going to kill myself. Anyone forced to live here would.*

Laughter tickled at his gut, and it felt good, even if it was the nervous kind. But mixed with the fading adrenaline in his system, it left him drained.

Grandma would help him. Grandma would understand. She always did.

Peter pressed the button to release the magnetic catch on the front door before pulling his hood up and stepping outside. Harsh winds tried to rip the hood from his head but held the tip and jogged to the car, rain bouncing off of his coat. With the keys shaking in his hand, Peter unlocked the door and jumped inside, his breath streaming away in smoke-like pillars. He started the engine and waited for it to warm, thinking of what he'd say when he reached his grandmother's. A half-hour drive to the farmhouse gave enough time to phrase it. Only a half hour, and then things would be better. This time he meant it, too.

This time, things would be different.

CHAPTER TWO

"Three days ago, I shit myself."

Mary shifted her position on the couch, watching her grandson with wide eyes. Peter continued.

"I did. I woke up and just felt it there. The worst part? I didn't even care. It didn't surprise me. Earlier, on my way home from work, you remember the coffee shop? I got a bottle of cheap whiskey with the last of my money. Hadn't eaten all day. I know I should have bought myself something for dinner, something to line my stomach, but I didn't. I was beyond feeling depressed, I suppose. Lower than low, you know? I'd reached out to Robbie and Bill. Stupid, right? Tried to convince them to meet with me, talk things over, maybe try get the band back on track. But they both said no. So, I bought a bottle of whiskey instead."

Mary's eyes glistened and she lifted a hanky to clear them. It hurt him to see her like this, but he needed to get it out, so he continued.

"I went home, put on the television, and downed the bottle in pretty much in one go. My throat and stomach burned but I kept drinking. I can't sleep anymore, so I needed to pass out or risk staying up all night with my head rotating the same bad thoughts again and again and again. I didn't just want to get drunk, I wanted to sleep and never wake up . . . Anyway, I remember gagging, and I remember my mouth salivating. You know how it happens right before you get sick? I leaned forward, like this, so I wouldn't puke on myself. I didn't puke. I must have made it to my bed instead, but I don't remember that part. I just remember waking up in my own mess. And ever since, I've been in a, a sort of a daze? Like watching myself in a movie or something. I needed to end it, Grandma."

Mary's voice was low and weak. "Peter, sweetheart, I can't take seeing you like this. I really can't. You were always so full of life, you know that? To hear you talk like this, telling me what you've done . . . I just don't know what to say." She reached across the coffee table and took a hold of his hands, her palms dry and hard. Beside them, their tea mugs steamed, untouched. "It's taken a lot of courage to come to me."

Here she goes again, Peter thought. *Justifying my actions. I'll always be the golden boy in her eyes. No matter what.*

"Grandma, I can't do this anymore. I need help—"

"And I'll give it to you, Peter."

"No, you don't understand. You've done too much for me already. When I got that apartment you practically paid for everything. I need to straighten myself out, once and for all. I need to go to rehab. I have to."

The old woman didn't reply, instead she leaned back and rubbed her hands together on her lap, letting him talk. Somewhere in the kitchen, a clock ticked.

"Beth was by."

"Beth?"

"Yes. She and I . . ."

Don't tell your grandmother about your sex life, you idiot . . .

"We . . . She's pregnant, Mary."

"Oh . . ." Mary looked about the room, not meeting his eyes. "Remember the day you gave me that?"

She pointed to the photograph of *Throttle* that hung above the fireplace. Peter's band. The center of attention. A young and healthy Peter smiled back from the picture, sandwiched between his drummer, Robert Greco, and his bass player, Bill Harris. All three of them looked so happy in the promotional shot for their debut album, and they were. The sky was their limit and people were paying attention to their music. *Throttle* was talked about all over the world. One of the best new rock bands to come out of York County. Their name was on everybody's tongue in the industry.

"I was so proud that day," Mary said. "So, so proud. Your mother would have been, too."

Peter swallowed down a lump in his throat. "She would have been, wouldn't she?"

"Of course she would have. You know, when we left Ireland and she was only a little thing, she said to me that one day she would do something amazing and make me proud. Moving to the U.S. flooded her imagination with possibilities. She had this look in her eye, this look of determination. And you know what? Like *most* other people, she wound up working an underpaid job that she hated. Remember Cleary's bar? Jesus. She *hated* it there. If they'd have taken a shot and promoted her to manager like she'd asked, she'd have turned it around, but they just wouldn't ever listen. Useless fecks. Too late now, anyway."

Peter sat forward. "I'm . . . I'm not sure what you're getting at?"

"She never felt *good* enough, Peter. Ever. And she'd tell me that. Always tell me that. But I just wanted her to be happy, that's all I ever wanted. No matter what she did, as long as she was happy, she was good enough to me. And when she had you, she was happy. She'd found her calling. She was a born-to-be mother and didn't even know it. She just wanted you to be happy, too. And when we lost her that night, Jesus, my heart still hurts just thinking about it . . . I know that all she'd want is for you to be happy. Going to this place, this rehab, it'll clean you up, won't it? And then you'll get in touch with Beth, that's what I'm understanding. Will that make you happy?"

"It would." Peter found it hard to talk. He cleared his throat. "I need to clean up my act. I'm a disappointment."

"Well you're not to me. You know that? People, good people, fall into problems with drugs all the time. And I'm not surprised, with all the rock and roll, I was half expecting it."

Peter smiled and tried to sound polite. "You know you always try and justify me? I'm a wallowing mess at the moment, Grandma. And as much as you don't want to hear it, I'm a bad person."

"No, you're a good person who made some bad choices. Want to know how I know? A bad person doesn't know they're bad. That's the difference. You have a conscience. And you're still so young. You're so handsome . . ." Tears spilled down her cheeks, patting on her blouse. "I knew about Bethany already. She called by yesterday. Wanted you to be the one to tell me so I waited for you to call. Then when you didn't, I went to call you. It was like magic, the phone just rang in my hands. She likes you an awful lot, you know that, right?"

Peter nodded. "Did she seem happy?"

"Ecstatic."

"I like her a lot, too."

The words seemed to come from somebody else's mouth as Peter slipped deeper in his own mind, replaying that fateful night over and over. Just as he did so many times lately. He'd gone to visit her on a Saturday, helping her move to her new apartment. Like Peter, Beth grew up an only child just outside the city, a neighbor of his grandmother's. They'd played together every day, just the two of them. No other kids their age lived out this way. In truth, she'd been his only real friend. And last month when he'd visited, their friendship finally took the next step, just as they knew it would. In the movies, their experience that night would have been magical, with music and a happy-ever-after ending, but in reality, it'd been a lot different. Peter spent the night sipping his beer and battling the urge to chug the whole case down his gullet. They'd played Monopoly, their favorite game from childhood, because Beth's TV hadn't been installed yet. Each time she won, Beth did a laugh that made Peter's sensitive stomach flutter. Then he'd kissed her.

Unlike a fairytale, they'd woken up the next morning a little embarrassed, awkward, and hung over. He'd left with a hug and a peck on the cheek.

After that, Peter had gone back to his nine-to-five coffee shop gig with nothing more than an incredible memory and a little hope for the future. Until that bottle of whiskey. Then he'd hated himself. In truth, he thought Beth far too good for him. She deserved more than he could ever hope to give. Beth deserved someone with their head screwed on, someone who knew how to cook exotic meals, say stimulating things, all that kind of stuff. Someone with a suit and tie and a million-dollar smile. Someone unlike him. Peter knew if Beth gave him a chance, he'd spend every day trying to hide his habits and fight his troubles. One day out of a month, maybe, he'd be able to do it (that night he'd only had four beers, after all), but a lifetime was out of the question. He couldn't risk Beth seeing him for what he truly was. A monster.

"... And now she's pregnant."

"What's that, dear?"

Peter shook his head. "Nothing. Just rambling."

Mary smiled, her lips trembling. "You're all I have, you know that? Jesus, what would I have done if you'd followed through with that stupid, *stupid* thing?"

The lump in Peter's throat came back like a lodged golf ball. "I know . . . I'm . . . Sorry."

"Promise me, promise me you won't do something like that again."

"I promise."

A solitary tear spilled down Mary's cheek. "You mean it?"

"Of course I do. I really am sorry, Grandma."

Peter stood and went to her. He wrapped his arms around her fragile figure and breathed her aroma, a pleasant mixture of lemon and lilac, possibly from her shower gel. The soft fabric of her blouse moved beneath his hands, and he squeezed her. "I'm so sorry." His voice came out muffled from her blouse. "I want to change."

"Then let's get you changed, Peter. For you, and for this child."

Mary pulled him back to arm's length and looked into his eyes. Her worn face was as rough as leather, but when she smiled, her face lit up. "You're going to make a great father. Even if you and Beth don't want to be an item, she knows that you'll be there for the kid. I know it, too. So let's get you cleaned up, okay? Tell me about this place."

Peter returned her smile. "I saw an advertisement in the back of the paper today. Never heard of a rehab center advertising, have you?"

Mary shook her head.

"Caught my attention. This place offers you a two-week detox course with group and personal support. From what I gathered, they give you jobs to do on this farm and you live and work there for the two weeks, talking to each other and getting counseling, working in the fresh air."

"You always liked working on the farm here, I think you'd enjoy it. And you *will* make a good father."

Peter smiled. His own father (a faceless sperm donor, nothing more—Grandmother's words, not his) left when he was a baby. Peter didn't know the man's name and was happy keeping it that way. He knew his mother, Karen, moved into his grandmother's place when she got pregnant and worked in a local bar just a short drive away to save money to get back on her feet. Because of that, she worked long hours, but Peter remembered her as a good mother. Caring. Until the icy night her car had skidded and—

"Are you okay, Peter?"

"Hmm? Yeah, I was just . . . Daydreaming."

"So what do we do now?"

"I . . ." The word caught in his throat. *Come on, Peter, just ask. You know it's the last time you will.* "I need to borrow some money."

The old woman didn't flinch, as Peter expected. "And?" She said. "How much?"

"I have five hundred, but that's only a quarter. I'd need a grand and a half to make up the rest . . ."

"Well then that's what we'll do. I'll give you the money, Peter, don't worry. And in two weeks, when you're out and clean and happy, we'll have dinner here and celebrate. Me, you, and Beth."

The thought of that day made Peter's head whirl. A day he'd be clean and happy and moving on with life? Hell, it might be possible.

"And what will you do after the detox place?" Mary asked. "Go back to the coffee shop?"

"No. I don't know what I'll do. At the minute I just want a fresh start, after that I don't know."

"So you need to call them, I guess. The detox place. Call and book a place?"

"I guess so. I'll need to get the time off work, too."

"But you're not going back there?"

"Good point."

The idea of never having to hand over another cardboard cup full of steaming hot muck to a too-busy-on-the-phone businessman at seven in the morning made him grin. He never understood how people drank that stuff, anyway. Coming from an Irish family, they were tea drinkers to the end, by God.

"Then I'll call and quit."

"Well, you know where the phone is. And Peter?"

"Yeah?"

"Call her, too. She'd like that. I'd imagine she's scared."

Peter nodded and crossed the room, the scent of baked bread drifting from the kitchen. Peter's stomach rumbled. His appetite had returned, it seemed.

Unfolding the torn piece of newspaper from his back pocket, Peter dialed the number shown. He didn't pause to think, in case he got cold feet.

The phone gave a solitary burr.

Maybe I should save up the money myself . . . But that could be months, and what if I take a drink?

A second ring.

Grandma would want me to take it, I can always pay her back when I'm clean and—

The phone buzzed a third time before being answered by a cheery, elderly man.

"Hello? Dawson Rehabilitation, Harris speaking."

"Hi . . ." Peter said, his mouth dry. "My name is Peter Laughlin, and I'd like to . . ."

. . . Commit myself? Send myself to? What phrase do I use here?

The old man chuckled with good nature. "You'd like to come to Dawson Rehabilitation, sir?"

"Yes, I would."

"That's not a problem, sir. How do you spell your name, please?"

Peter spelled it out. They talked for ten more minutes while the old man filled him in on the logistics and details of the center. Dawson Rehabilitation, he said, operated from a small work-office in New York City and was owned by Doctor Harris Dawson, a renowned psychologist and well regarded counselor. As Peter found out, it was him personally on the phone.

"My partner, Jerry Fisher," Dawson explained, "is the man you'll be dealing with on the retreat. Like me, he is a counselor with a very good history to his name, and that you can research for yourself, should you have any concerns. Jerry is forty-five years young, you see, and because of that he is much, much more suited to the manual labor you'll be doing on the farmhouse than myself." The old man wheezed a laugh and Peter smiled to himself. He'd be lying if he said he didn't feel good for making the call. "We have two more places available for the course," Dawson said. "Once they're filled, should be later today or tomorrow going by the other calls, we'll be in touch and give you our set date. Does that sound okay?"

"Yes. That sounds fine."

"Any more questions, Mr. Laughlin? Please, don't be afraid to ask."

"Could you tell me more about this farm?"

"Of course." The old man cleared his throat. "The Dawson farmhouse is located in the woodlands of Pennsylvania. In fact, believe it or not, it used to be my family home. I'll admit I'm not much of a country buff, Mr. Laughlin, so I leased it year-in year-out while I moved to New York and got the business off the ground. It was always my idea to use it for Dawson Rehab as a center for retreats, and I'm glad that I now get to."

"Sounds nice."

"It is. The main house is a two-story, beautiful old place with a good-sized porch out front. The trees have been felled and cleared, leaving a very nice yard I plan to get graveled soon enough. I think you'll enjoy your time there, Mr. Laughlin."

"Thank you, Dr. Dawson."

"My pleasure. Please, call me Harris. I'll be in touch. And good luck, Peter. Welcome to the Dawson Rehabilitation program."

Peter lowered the phone to the cradle and took a deep breath. He'd done it, and he felt better than he had in weeks. He was going to be a dad, after all. Not just a biological father, a goddamn good dad.

Mary smiled from the living room doorway. "All done?"

"All done, Grandma."

She shuffled over and gave him a hug. "I'm proud of you. You know that."

Peter placed his head on her shoulder and squeezed back.

"Now, call *her*," Mary said. "Please."

Without another word, his grandmother shuffled to the kitchen. Peter heard the radio come to life and the old woman humming to some country music. He lifted the phone for a second time and dialed Beth's number. He knew it by heart.

"Hello?"

"Beth?"

"Peter!" She sounded relieved. "I've wanted to talk to you."

"I know." Hearing her voice, tension drifted from Peter's body. All of his troubles dissolved. "I'm at my grandma's place."

Beth sniffled, sounding as if she'd started to cry but still happy. "And? How are you? I've been worried about you."

"I feel amazing, Beth." His own voice cracked with the weight of the words. He cleared his throat. "I really do. Honestly. Beth, I want to do this. Be a dad . . . Will you let me?"

Beth sighed. "You have no idea how much I wanted to hear you say that. I've been so frightened, thinking I'll do this alone, or if I can't then going and getting it removed and . . . I've been so *scared*."

"I know, I know. Look, I have to go somewhere for the next two weeks, but when I'm back, I'm here for good. I'll be here for you, okay? We'll do this together."

"I'm so relieved you called."

"Beth . . . We'll take our time, all right? We'll do this right. I promise you."

"I know."

Peter let comfortable silence sink in, listening to her breathing. Then Beth said something that sent his world away. "I love you."

Without hesitating, Peter said it back. They talked for fifteen minutes, and with each passing moment, Peter couldn't believe the events of that morning had happened to the same man. Afterwards, they said their goodbyes, and Peter returned the receiver to its cradle.

"I better get going, Grandma," he shouted into the kitchen. "I need to get home and pack."

"Of course. I love you, Peter."

"I love you, too."

She shuffled from the kitchen drying her hands in a towel, and he kissed her head before opening for the door. Outside, the wind still screeched and the dark sky poured rain. Peter dashed for his car and climbed inside, shivering at the cold. His grandmother stood in the doorway and waved, pulling her blouse tight across her chest. Peter honked the horn as he pulled out of the driveway, giving one final wave back.

Today's the start of a new life, he told himself. *If I can keep it together.*

CHAPTER THREE

"Peter Laughlin, I take it?"

"Yes, sir."

Peter shook the hand of the large man addressing him. By his looks, Peter guessed him to be ex-military. Cropped hair sat slack from the rain against his thick skull. Despite his mean appearance, however, the man gave a polite smile before releasing his calloused grip.

"Jerry Fisher," he said. "It's a pleasure. Now, I just need to double check everybody's here before we take off."

As Jerry looked to the clipboard, Peter took in the area. The clouds had finally broke that morning and rain blew down in sheets, sounding like radio static as it hit the tarmac. Harris Dawson had called the night before, asking Peter if he'd make his way to a shopping center car park in the city center for nine a.m. Missing the alarm, he'd just about made it. Now, family cars littered the lot, the navy-blue eight seater bus they were about to take sticking out among them.

Jerry Fisher tapped a pen on his clipboard. "Henry Randolph?"

"Here."

Henry raised his hand, an old man hunched against the harsh weather. A whisk of thin hair clung to his damp skull, blowing in the wind. Dark circles drooped beneath his eyes. The dark green raincoat he wore looked made of oil in the rain. He reminded Peter of an animal who'd seen too much abuse, now cautious of others.

"Good," Jerry said. "Walter Cartwright?"

"H-here."

The chunky middle-aged man shuffled about from foot to foot as if he needed to pee. His thick-framed glasses, dotted with raindrops, sat crooked on his nose. Badly dyed, black hair circled his head from temple to temple with a perfectly round bald spot to top it off. He gave a lopsided grin as the gathering turned to him. "H-Hello. Walter, Walter Cartwright. It's a pleasure."

Jerry nodded. "It's nice to meet you, Walter. Jamie Peters?"

"Yeah."

Peter looked to the kid, the kind of person who would've dunked Peter's head in the toilet if they'd attended the same school. But despite the jock's youthful appearance, dark circles beneath his eyes aged him by a decade. An addict, Peter could tell, and most likely to prescription drugs. Everything Peter had been at seventeen, this kid seemed the opposite.

Except here, Peter thought, *he's in the same boat as you. So cut him some slack.*

"Shelly Matthews?"

A mousy voice spoke up. "Yes."

Peter placed the woman at about forty-five, showing telltale signs of a time-hardened junkie. Her actual age was probably closer to thirty. She rubbed at deep scratch marks lining her bare arms, shivering. "I've only got a tee shirt, Mr. Fisher. Can we get going soon? Don't wanna catch a cold."

"Of course," Jerry said. "Apologies, Shelly. Just one more. Donald Bove?"

"Right here."

Jesus Christ, Peter thought. *What is this guy? Mafia?*

If Peter learned that Donald Bove starred in the movie *The Godfather*, it would not have surprised him. The man wore a long leather trench coat that glistened in the rain. Comb lines ran the length of his slicked-back hair.

Ah! Peter thought. *Got it. A younger, fatter Robert De Niro.*

Jerry tucked away his clipboard and clapped his hands. "Okay, we're all accounted for. Rain's starting to really come down now, so if you'd all like to climb aboard the bus, we'll get moving. Sorry for our late start, and it's a pleasure to meet you all."

Donald Bove went first, clamoring inside and taking the front seat. The nervous fat man named Walter Cartwright followed but stood aside to allow Henry Randolph onboard. "After you, sir."

The old man climbed in without a word, his face long and unreadable. He went to the back of the bus.

Walter smiled and gave a nod to the group. "Ma'am, you, too."

"Thanks Walter."

Shelly Matthews took a set at the front of the bus, hugging her skeletal frame and looking out the window. Peter went next, taking the seat behind Shelly and Donald and Walter shuffled after, taking the seat next to him. Jamie came last.

"Peter, is it?"

A cold, wet hand engulfed his and Peter shook despite his revulsion. "Yeah. It's nice to meet you, Walter."

"What brings you to this retreat?" Walter's magnified eyes jittered over Peter. "What's your vice? Or is that too personal? Oh, I shouldn't have asked."

Peter smiled. "Not to worry. Little bit of this, little of that. Mainly booze."

"Ah. I see, I see."

"And you?"

Walter sighed and wiped his glasses on his soaked shirt. "Prescription medications. I mean, my doctor knows I'm not the most stable man in the world, but he put me on these anti-depressants about a year ago. And it just sort of . . . Got out of hand. Spiraled. My mood went all over the place. Soon enough, I was balancing uppers with downers and uppers with downers and . . . Well, you get the idea. Had a wife, now I don't. You know how it goes."

"Sure," Peter said. He didn't, not the loss of a partner, but he wasn't in the mood to have a heart to heart with Walter Cartwright. That could be saved for group support sessions, which he assumed there would be many of. In fact, if Peter was honest, he'd never had any type of relationship before. With *Throttle* active, the band had eaten up his time with recording, touring and rehearsing. Of course, there had been girls on the road, but that grew tiresome faster than it'd been fun. When the band broke up, the bottle had been there for him. He'd been in no condition to care for another human being. Hell, he'd hardly been responsible to care for himself.

Peter gave Walter a smile before buckling his seatbelt and turning his attention to the window. Out there, the world went on, normal as ever. Talkative, happy folk went about their day, walking their pets, doing their shopping, visiting loved ones, all sorts of things that normal, capable people do. Peter wondered if they knew their luck, something as simple as getting through a standard day without getting black-out drunk. He envied them, because the bus oozed despair. He could feel it, an almost tangible sense, like a dark mist constricting the group. An unseen boa of addiction.

"Well, we're all set," Jerry Fisher called from up front. He keyed the ignition and the bus vibrated. A happy, morning time chat-show chimed from the radio. "We'll be about an hour or so on the road. I hope you've all used the bathroom."

A few lighthearted chuckles greeted this, but Peter felt like a child on a school trip being chaperoned by a responsible adult. He half expected to be asked to 'buddy-up' as not to get lost. His stomach jerked as the bus set off.

What have I gotten myself into? Peter's heart quickened. His palms grew sweaty. *Just what have I gotten myself into?*

Walter patted his leg, making him jump. "Hey. It's all right. We're all in this together, okay? We'll be like a family. You'll get through this."

Peter sighed and closed his eyes, the bus rocking him back and forth. The sound of the radio fell away. Very soon, he drifted into asleep.

He saw a packed stadium, the stage decked with a lighting rig and colossal PA. The deafening sound of applause erupted from the crowd. He'd seen this place before, San Francisco in 2010. The debut record, *Broken Dreams,* had just cracked the top ten. Squished against a metal barrier at the front of the stage stood a wall of sweating fans, their eyes searching the platform. Peter stood alone with no sign of Robby or Bill, an acoustic guitar hanging from his neck. His stomach roiled with nerves. How could he break it to so many people that the band no longer together existed? How would they react? Blinded by the stage lights, Peter raised his hand against their sharp glare. He pressed his lips to the microphone and cleared his throat. A squeal of feedback followed.

"Hi, everyone. I know you were expecting—"

Peter's voice caught in his throat. His heart jackhammered his chest. Staring back weren't the eyes of fans like in San Francisco. Instead, he found himself looking into glazed-over faces of the dead. They slouched and drooled, their flesh slopping away and hitting the floor. Their hands left brown streak marks on the barrier. Their stench hit, overwhelming, like rancid meat. Then Peter heard their chanting.

"*Join us, join us, join us . . .*"

Someone tapped his shoulder and Peter snorted, bolting upright. "Hmm?"

The bus pottered along an old country road, the engine angry as it climbed a steep hill. Thick redwoods enclosed the road from either side, making it seem like nighttime instead of the middle of the day.

Walter stuck his face in Peter's. "Wake up, sleepy head. We're almost there. You've been out the whole way. Nearly two hours, in fact."

"Oh." Peter rubbed at his eyes. "Thanks, Walter."

Shifting his position, Peter eyed the isolated road. Deep woodlands stretched as far as the eye could see. A startled fox bolted from behind one of the bushes and shot across the road, leaping into a thicket. Now and then the gray sky cut through the fat tangle of leaves overhead, strobing light on the window. Rain drummed the roof.

"Just here, folks," Jerry Fisher called from up front. "If you'd like to look out your window, the farmhouse should be coming into view any second now."

As bus rounded a sharp corner, the building slipped into sight. A large, two-story farmhouse, just as Harris Dawson had said. On a good day, Peter imagined the place would look idyllic with its large open porch and smoking chimney. In his mind's eye, he could see the dark wood turn a golden brown from the setting sun. But now, gray clouds cluttered the sky, and instead of homey, the place looked like a nightmare escapee. The home of an inbred *Addams Family*.

A single redwood stood in the yard, and around it, the grass yellowed, balding away to mud in patches. A cat slept on the steps of the porch. With the amount of money the clients paid,

Peter thought the place would be a little more visually welcoming, but then again, he thought, they were here to work, not to relax.

The bus rattled up the driveway, passing a single band of barbed wire dripping with rainwater. In the mud beneath the wire, Peter noted a thick white line also circling the yard. Subtle, but there.

"You see that?" Walter asked. "In the mud. There."

"Salt," Peter said, squinting. "Keeps the slugs away from crops . . . But I don't see any vegetation in the yard, just . . . Dirt."

"Right." Walter produced a battered notebook and began scribbling. "Slugs don't like salt . . . But eat their veggies. They like those, do they?"

"Yes, Walter. They do."

"All right," Jerry said. "We're here. I'd advise you get on your jackets if you have them, looks like the sky's about to really open up again."

The bus crept to a stop outside the porch and Jerry killed the engine, silencing the radio and startling the cat. Rain beat the rooftop like tiny drumming fingers and a single stream of water slopped down Peter's window, blurring the outdoors.

Jerry opened his door. "Out we go."

Pulling his suitcase from beneath his seat, Peter waited for the others to climb out. He listened to their boots slosh the mud as they ran for the house, dragging their suitcases, then he stood.

"Hey."

Peter turned. The old man, Henry, sat alone in the back of the bus.

"Um, hi. Henry, was it?"

The old man nodded. "Listen, kid . . . I . . ." He took a deep breath. "I'm scared. Can I tell you that?"

Peter sat. "Of course. If it makes you feel any better, I am, too."

Henry flashed a smile. "I've a bad feeling about this."

"I know how you feel, man. But we'll get through, don't worry. We'll all help each other out. I mean, we're all here for the same reason."

The old man's eyes went to the window, his bushy brows

drawn together. "Nah. It's this place. Makes me anxious. I feel . . . Off."

"Think we were both expecting a little more hospitality for our money, that's all. It might not be the Hilton, but it'll clean us out, that's the main part. Come on, we'll get inside and suss it out. New environment, takes a while to settle in, you know?"

Henry didn't reply.

"All right. I'll see you inside, man."

Peter made his way off the bus, slipping as he slung his suitcase over his shoulder. The mud sucked at his boots and he pulled against it, plodding to the house. In the shelter of the porch, he shivered.

"Shoes, if you don't mind, Mr. Laughlin."

"Sure thing, Jerry."

Jerry gave a brisk nod before returning inside while Peter removed his muddy footwear.

Off to a good start, Peter thought. *At least I didn't punch him.*

The heat of the farmhouse prickled Peter's arms as he placed his suitcase on the floor. He chuckled.

Good thing I didn't judge too soon. This place isn't bad . . . Not bad at all.

A thick red carpet covered the staircase ahead. To the left stood two doors, both deep mahogany, and both closed. Small metal name-holders embossed the wood, the kind found on a doctor's door. Peter squinted, making out '*living room*' and '*dining room/kitchen*'. A large set of double doors also flanked the right, the name holder too far to read, but Peter guessed it to be a library.

Two men stood to either side of the staircase. The man on the right wore a tartan shirt with the sleeves rolled halfway up his meaty arms. His thick, ginger beard lifted as he flashed a tight smile to the newcomers. To the left of the stairs, a skinny black man wearing a plain work shirt gave a wave and rocked on the heels of his feet, his freshly shaved head bouncing light off an overhead chandelier.

"Let me get that for you," the first man said and reached for Peter's suitcase. Peter thanked him as he put it with the others by the stairs.

"Ah, you're all in. Good." Jerry Fisher came from the dining-room, dabbing at his hair with a towel, a bundle tucked beneath his arm. "Here, take one each. Dry up."

As the group patted themselves down, Jerry motioned to the two men. "I'd like you all to meet Andrew Harper and Paul Richardson. They are our staff, and both are here to help you with anything you should need. Do not be afraid to talk to them."

The two men nodded.

"Now, while Andrew and Paul bring your bags to your rooms, please join me in the living room. I've prepared some refreshments, and you can warm by the fire. Please, come, get cozy."

The scent of pine hung thick in the living room, a spacious area with a full-length window. Peter saw the yard through the buffered glass, the yellowing grass stretching to the wired-off woodlands. Ahead in the room, a roaring fire cast dancing shadows along the polished hardwood. Two plush couches surrounded an oak table in the center of the room, a white rug resting beneath its feet. Ten mugs circled a steaming metal pot on top of the table. The smell of cocoa ghosted beneath the scent of pine.

"It's a very nice room, Jerry," Walter said. "Very big. Very, very nice."

"I'm glad you like it, Mr. Cartwright." He faced to the group. "Please, make yourselves at home."

Peter took a seat, scooting close to the fire. He removed his raincoat and folded it on the armrest while Jamie Peters, the young athletic man, sat next to him.

"I'm glad you're all here," Jerry said, ladling out cocoa into each of the cups. "I want you to feel relaxed, and at home. This is a non-judgmental environment. When we start our group sessions together, I want you to feel safe and secure, as if you were talking to family. Because that's what we're going to be over the next two weeks. Like a family."

Jerry handed a mug to Peter with a smile. The warmth worked into Peter's hands.

"For tonight, please relax. Feel free to get familiar with the house and roam about. Across the hallway is the library—"

Bingo!

"—Which is connected to my study, and I'd request it to be the only room out of bounds for obvious reasons, but there's a TV room next door with a DVD player and good selection of movies. You're more than welcome to use it. We don't have cable here. I do have to set a curfew on the television watching, however, so as not to disturb our other guests. How does eleven p.m. sound?"

Nobody responded.

"Okay, then. Eleven it is." Jerry finished doling out the cups. "You'll need to keep a regular sleep pattern to keep your strength up. We'll be having breakfast at eight, followed by our first group session at nine. At ten o'clock we'll begin our work on the farm. Anybody who doesn't like manual labor is free to take up another task, all I ask is you try your best to cooperate. We're all here to get through a very, very rough patch, and we'll work hard to do just that. I promise you, we *will* do this."

Walter cleared his throat. "Thank you for your hospitality, Jerry." He dipped a chubby finger into his cocoa, stirring. "It's so nice. I haven't been treated with such kindness for a long, long time. In fact, I can't even remember the last time someone was so nice to me." Walter sniffled, a tear dropping to his lap. "It's been so hard," he said, shaking. "So very hard." Cocoa slopped to his lap. His lips quivered. "Nobody seems to like me, because I'm a *loser*. A big stinking loser." His voice rose. "I'm a big stinking loser! I'm a big stinking lo—"

Jerry moved fast and kneeled beside him. "Walter, hey, Walt, it's all right. You're here now. You're not a loser. You're not. You're going to change."

"I'm never going to *change*!"

With that, he stood and hurled the mug, shattering it against the far wall. Jerry grabbed his shoulders, forcing him back down. "Sit, Walter. *Shhhh* . . . Sit."

"I'm sorry, Jerry, I don't know what happened."

Donald Bove slapped the couch, making Peter jump. He stood. "That shit ain't okay!" He shot Walter a look of repulsion. "Crazy fat bastard just threw a damn mug! He gonna take one of our heads off next? What is this, a fuckin' nut house?"

Jerry raised his palms. "Mr. Bove, please. We're here to support each other. Try and be a little more understanding. Cope."

"Yeah," Walter spat, his face red. "We're going to cope, Mr. Bove, we are!"

"Doing a great job there, Walter."

Walter covered his face like a child hiding. Peter watched with genuine shock and amusement. Jerry pulled at Walters hands. "Let it out. *Shhh* . . . Mr. Bove, Donald, try and be more sympathetic, okay? When your time comes and you need to let something out, you're going to need us as your family. Not as your enemies."

That seemed to get through. Donald stared at the floor, flexing his jaw.

"Thank you," Jerry said. "Now, please apologize to Mr. Cartwright."

"Say what?"

Water's face reappeared. "Yeah! Say you're sorry!"

The room turned to Donald.

"Say you're sorry!"

An uncomfortable quiet settled, and the group waited, Peter's stomach jumping with butterflies.

"I'm . . . I'm sorry, all right?" Donald said. "*Jeeesus.*"

Snot and tears crawled down Walter's face. "*Thank* you."

"Okay," Jerry said. "Walter, sit back down and I'll have Paul or Andrew clean up the mess, don't worry about it."

Walter's face fell. "Oh god, I'm so sorry, I threw your mug!"

"It's *okay*, just sit down and get comfortable."

"Okay. Sorry everybody. I'm real sorry."

"S'all right, man," Shelly said, moving aside as Walter took a seat. She smiled to him, legitimate but sad. Her voice sounded harsh from what Peter guessed were many years of chain-smoking. "I'm sure we're all going to break down at some point. Even us who seem to be made out of stone, right? That's what we're here for, after all. To get it all out." She squeezed his shoulder.

And that's when fear crept through Peter. He hadn't considered what might come out of *him* yet. What had *he* pent up inside?

Peter took even breaths, trying to remain calm as Jerry said, "We'll save what we can for our first discussion tomorrow morning. Don't be afraid to cry."

Those words didn't help, because Peter didn't know that once he did cry, he could ever stop. How deep did his problem go? He never had a proper look. Now, he had no choice.

The first night at the Dawson farmhouse began.

CHAPTER FOUR

Peter worked his bare feet into the rug on the bedroom floor, listening as the rain rapped the window. Through the floorboards came the soft sound of the television from the room below. If Fisher hadn't taken their mobile devices with the claim that they might '*talk to the wrong kinds of people,*' he would have crushed candies or read the news, anything to distract himself and pass the time. His suitcase sat on the end of the bed, the only piece of furniture in the room other than the chest of drawers beside it. Somewhere in the hallway, a grandfather clock ticked.

Moving the suitcase aside, Peter sat on the bed. A hard mattress, just as he liked. Each of the guests at the Dawson farmhouse had been given their own room on the second floor and, luckily, Peter's came equipped with an en suite bathroom. From what he'd heard, the Dawson farmhouse had been converted some years ago to accommodate the doctor's business. Harris Dawson had renovated the upstairs, chopping the once large study into five smaller rooms that the guests now occupied.

Someone knocked on the door.

"Yes?"

"Peter, it's Jerry Fisher. May I come in?"

"Yes."

Jerry opened the door and stepped inside. A pair of reading glasses softened his otherwise hard face. He smiled.

"Everything all right? You settled in?"

"I'm fine. Thanks, Jerry. Think I just need a good night sleep."

"I hope Walter's little outburst didn't startle you earlier. That type of behavior isn't easy to watch."

Peter nodded. "What do you think happened, exactly?"

"A breakdown." Those two words hung heavy in the air. "Look, I'm sorry for earlier, Peter. But it happens more than you'd imagine. People who come in to a place like this are very emotionally charged, like sticks of lit dynamite just waiting for the fuse to burn out. And when it does, it's not nice, but it's perfectly natural, and is the first part of what it takes to get better. Acceptance to the problem has already begun, I mean, that's why you're all here. But realizing this new reality can be hard to take. Walter's not a bad man, Peter, he's sick. He needs help. And that's what we're here for."

Peter nodded again. He supposed he shouldn't be so hard on Walter. After all, the very same thing could happen to him. Or perhaps worse.

Jerry flashed a smile. "Sleep well, Peter. Paul will be around to wake you at seven-thirty. If you have any problems during the night, a buzzer's clipped beneath your bed. It sends a signal to Andrew's room. He's on night duty, should you need anything."

"Okay. Will do."

"Sleep well."

Jerry left and eased the door shut, followed by the muffled sound of him knocking the next room.

A cigarette, Peter thought. *Probably have to go to the front porch.*

Unzipping his bag, he rooted inside the front pouch. Before meeting Jerry and the group at the car park, he'd stocked up on Marlboros in the shopping center. Enough for two weeks. Now his fingers found nothing but flint and fluff.

"Jerry?" His voice sounded too loud in the small room. His heartbeat quickened. "Jerry?"

A muffled voice came from the next room, followed by Jerry's too-slow footsteps. He reappeared in the doorway. "Yes, Peter? What can I do for you?"

Peter worked his jaw. "My cigarettes. They're gone."

Jerry took a moment before lacing his fingers together. "Mr. Laughlin, we're here to help you detox. To cleanse your body. Cigarettes are not allowed in Dawson Rehabilitation. They'll be returned to you at the end of the two weeks. When you get them, it'll be your choice to do as you will, but I sincerely hope you won't take them."

Peter's voice rose against his will. "That should have been stated a little more clearly, Jerry. You can't do that, man. It's not an institution, I chose to be here."

"And I'm helping you. Please, see it from my perspective. I'm doing this for you and—"

"Oh fuck you and the horse you rode in on."

Where the hell had that one come from?

Peter muttered an unsteady laugh and rubbed his forehead. "You're right. You're absolutely right. You're just trying to help. I apologize."

"Apology accepted, Peter." Jerry nodded with a grin and placed a hand on the door. "Now get some sleep. I'll see you in the morning."

The door clicked shut and Peter took a deep breath. He knew Jerry was right, of course, but it didn't help matters. His brain screamed for nicotine, sending bolts of electricity through his core.

"Fuck." Peter clasped the back of his neck. He didn't have to like this. Some tough love was in order, but that wasn't easy to accept.

I'll still go downstairs, he thought. *Get some fresh air. That'll help.*

When had been the last time he'd gone without a cigarette? He recalled a three day bet with Robby Greco, his drummer. Robby'd said no way in hell Peter Laughlin, *the* Peter Laughlin, could go five minutes without a pull. Of course, Robby'd *slightly* exaggerated, but still made a good point. Peter remembered slamming his finished beer on the table and accepting the challenge for twenty dollars each. Not a whole lot, but he'd have done it for free, anyway. And do it he did. But holy fuck, what a frightening three days those had been. He usually had one cigarette per hour, and when that first hour passed, he'd been in for a shock. He felt lightheaded. His mind forced his fingers to curl, holding a phantom smoke, unable to think of anything else. He sweated, his head feeling like a helium balloon. It was at that moment he realized just how deep the hook of addiction had taken a hold. And after the initial craving passed, he decided to see the bet through, to prove to himself, and Robby, that he had the will power to do so. After the first day, he developed cold-like symptoms. His nose ran nonstop, leaking like a sprung tap. That'd been the oxygen returning to his system. He'd slept badly, tossing and turning and sweating and cursing, but the next day went a little easier. He still felt lightheaded and confused, but it'd been manageable. On the third day, laughing with Robby that he did it, he took a smoke and went straight back to ground zero. Just like he'd never quit.

That'd been cigarettes, He thought. *And for only three days. They're just a footnote to the booze this time . . . When's the last time you even* slept *sober?*

Passing the television room, Peter watched the glow seeping around the doorframe like ectoplasm. Later, a movie might help, he decided. Something to distract himself. He moved on and let himself outside, grimacing at the cold.

"Hello."

"Oh, hey." Peter closed the door and stuffed his hands inside his pockets. "Henry, right?"

The old man sat on the rocking chair with his hands clasped. He stared out into the rain, his face set. In his eyes, Peter saw sadness.

"You mind if I take a seat?"

Peter nodded to the bench by the rocking chair but the old man didn't respond. Instead, he took a deep breath and continued to stare out into darkness. A harsh wind blew and Peter shuddered. "Okay. Well I'm going to go ahead and sit."

Peter lowered himself, his eyes trained on the old man. The bench creaked beneath him, the cold wood freezing his ass, but he didn't want to move now that he'd gone this far. He had said he was going to sit, so damn it, he was going to sit.

The rain sounded like static as it hit the muddy surface of the farmyard. In the distance, cloaked in darkness, thick clouds passed above the silhouetted treetops.

"So," Peter said. "Just found out they took my cigarettes. Had a whole mess of 'em stocked up in my luggage. Fisher told me, with a smile I might add, that they're all gone. *Poof*. . . Wanted to punch his stupid face."

That got a smirk. Then the old man's face returned to stone.

"Ah, you don't like Jerry either?"

Henry only blinked, clearing his throat. Smiling, Peter leaned back on the bench despite its cold. "Ah, he's all right, you know? Just doing his job, even if he comes across a little condescending. I mean, maybe we are childish, right? Maybe we need some tough love. Well, maybe not you. I know nothing about you."

Peter let the invitation dangle a moment, waiting for Henry to bite but only got more silence.

Christ, am I talking to a damn statue?

"Okay then." Peter leaned forward. "Guess I'm Jack Nicholson and you're the Indian."

"Randal McMurphy."

"Huh?"

Henry rubbed his hands together, making a noise like sandpaper. "The character's name was Randal McMurphy."

Peter arched his eyebrows. Judging by the accent, Henry was from up north, perhaps Maine. In a gruff and weathered voice he added, "I was twelve when that novel came out, you know. Not the movie. In nineteen-sixty-two. Bought it with the money I'd made raking neighbors' yards and doin' odd jobs around my hometown. Read that thing cover to cover in a single sitting. Ken Kesey was a terrific writer. The novel is told through Chief Bromden's perspective, did you know that? I might not like this place, but at least the staff aren't The Combine."

"The what?"

The old man sniffled. "Never mind. I found the Native American stories particularly interesting."

"Is that right?"

"And Ken Kesey, from what I hear, never liked that Jack Nicholson got cast as Randal McMurphy. In the novel, Mac's a burly Irish-American. Red-haired."

"Is that right? Interesting."

Henry leaned forward, eyeing the rain. "Guess that makes Jerry Fisher our own nurse Ratched, doesn't it?"

Peter snorted and clapped his hands. "Suppose it does, man, suppose it does. And what about you? Did he take your cigarettes?"

"Perky bastard took every pack I had. And my phone. I'd be destroying candies right now if I had it."

"Ah, you play, too? Shit. It's tough, huh? I can't remember the last time I went without one. A cigarette."

Peter settled into the bench, his body adjusting to the temperature. Visible air ran from his nose and mouth, not unlike cigarette smoke. He got an idea.

"Hey, remember when you were a kid in school, winter time? Absolutely freezing out. Some smart-ass kid would pretend to smoke? Remember? He'd cup his hand to his mouth, blow cold air. Like this . . ." Peter demonstrated. "All exaggerated like. And he'd shout, '*I'm smoking, look, I'm smoking!*'"

Henry raised an eyebrow, turning to face Peter. A smile played on his weathered face. "What you getting at?"

"Well, Henry, would you like a cigarette?"

Routing inside his pocket, Peter removed an invisible carton of smokes and presented them. "You're in luck, I've only got two left, but I have a whole mess of 'em back in my room. We're golden for the rest of the two weeks. Hope you like Marlboro."

The old man kept his eye on Peter, all the while removing a not-so-there cigarette from the invisible box. Peter did the same. Bringing the pretend cigarette to his lips, he made a clicking sound, then he inhaled the cold night air deep into his lungs, exhaling it slow. The air flew away in a thick cloud, and for all the wonders of the world, it relaxed him.

"That's better."

Chuckling, Henry brought his own cigarette to his mouth. "This is ridiculous."

He clicked his lips and inhaled, then, with his mouth puckered, blew away the smoke. The wind carried it off towards the woods. "You know, for whatever reason, it actually feels good."

Peter laughed. "I know, right? Must be the action with your hands or something. The habit."

"Right."

They sat in silence and sucked cold air, watching the fuzzy sheet of rain patter onto the muddy yard.

"You see that?" Henry asked. "I've been sitting here for a good half hour, trying to figure it out."

"See what?"

Peter strained his eyes, followed the old man's gaze into the yard. He shook his head. "Don't see anything."

"The mist."

"Well, I see *that*. Fog. It's pretty thick."

A fat cloud clung the ground, swirling as the rain sliced through. It swallowed the entire yard, rendering it impossible to see beyond a few feet. Past the bus, the grounds faded into an almost solid fog.

"There's just something strange about it," Henry said. "Can't quite put my finger on it . . . I've watched it for ages, trying to figure it out, but I can't."

"Maybe your mind's playing tricks, happens. Having a hard time adapting to this place."

"Perhaps."

Peter decided to change the subject. "What was your choice of poison, by the way? If you don't mind my asking."

"Liquor."

"Booze? Me, too."

"Strong liquor."

"I see. Whiskey?"

The old man sighed. "And brandy. They were my Achilles' heel. It got so bad in the past year I easily downed at least a bottle a day. The brandy made me feel bad, though. Thins the blood out, gets the heart pumping. Not good for high blood pressure. Or the fact that weak hearts run in the family. Guaranteed way of getting a stroke if you don't get it under control. Surprised my ticker hasn't spluttered out already. Half expecting it any day now."

"Right . . . I was a whiskey and beer guy."

"Never could stand the taste of beer. Piss water."

Peter pressed his lips together. "You know, I never knew if I actually liked the taste myself. Just grew to crave it. Same as nicotine, especially in the last three years or so. When that happens, you know you've got a problem. I didn't want to admit it. Forced myself not to see what it was doing to me."

"I know. Funny how we fool ourselves until it's too late. Then there's no taking it back."

Peter decided not to press the matter further. Whatever happened to Henry, or whatever the old man had done, played on the old man's mind. Peter could tell from his eyes.

When he wants to speak, he'll speak. Can't deny I'm not curious.

Henry looked to him, his deep blue eyes glistening in the overhead light. "Well, if I stay here any longer I'll freeze to death. You, too. Don't think you're invincible just because you're young. Get inside." He motioned to the yard. "Besides, that fog's getting on my nerve."

"Sure thing."

They both stood, Henry wincing as his back popped. "Bones can't take the cold," He said. "Got worse in the last couple years. Fingers are getting painful when I try and play, I just hope it's not arthritis."

Peter paused. "Try and play? Music?"

"Yes. Play the banjo, recreationally. Had dreams of taking it up professionally when I was younger, but they're big dreams for a small man. Never had the courage."

Peter's heart raced. "I play, too, you know." *Play*, he thought. *That's the wrong word.* He corrected himself. "*Played.* I played. I used to be a guitarist."

"Were you any good?"

"I was all right. But that's a story for another day."

"You have a band?"

"Had. *Throttle.*" Saying the name to an elderly person sounded silly. "Yeah, we were a rock band."

"Huh. Never heard of you."

"Guessed as much."

Henry opened the front door, amplifying tin-can laughter from the TV room, and Peter stepped inside. The warmth felt like a shot of whiskey on a cold night. "What room are you in?" he asked.

Henry closed the door. "Right across from you, I believe. You're to the left there?"

"Yeah. First room."

"Got your own bathroom?"

"Luckily."

"Me, too. I have a kidney infection so I'm up pissing at least four times a night. It's disgusting. I didn't have one, I'd need one."

"I hear you."

Peter respected the old man's honesty, found it refreshing. He hadn't met someone like that in a long time, someone he could talk to. Lately, his public interaction seemed to be nothing but formal pleasantries.

"Well," he said. "Sleep well, Henry. See you in the morning."

"Sure thing. You take it easy . . . Patrick, was it?"

"Pete. Peter. But close enough."

"Yeah, yeah I know, just kidding. Don't get to do that much anymore. People seem to either pity or hate me."

"Tell me about it."

They made their way upstairs, Peter keeping pace with the old man. After parting ways and a final word, Peter turned off his light and lay on the bed. The fresh white sheets smelt of fabric softener, and lacing his fingers behind his head, Peter closed his eyes with a sigh. The nicotine craving had passed, but he knew it would be back again. It always was. The talk had distracted him, at least, but now he needed to try and sleep.

Peter's eyes twitched beneath their lids as from the hallway, the grandfather clock sounded louder and louder. His hands tightened.

Tick . . . Tock . . . Tick . . . Tock . . .

Peter took a long, shuddering breath and released it slow as beads of sweat formed on his forehead.

"*It's all right.* I can do this. I can do this, stop worrying."

He imagined the sensation of a cold beer racing towards his stomach, cooling his parched throat, bubbles fizzing. He'd take half the can in two mouthfuls, then belch in victory. How satisfying, to take the edge off things, like a warm blanket tossed over the brain. In another five minutes, he'd have the second half of the can gone. Then, with a pull of the tab, another would be opened and waiting, beckoning him, the weight good in his hand. He'd repeat, and repeat, and repeat . . .

Peter pinched the bridge of his nose and let out a sigh. His hands shook.

"*. . . I'm so fucking scared.*"

Then the screaming started, coming from down the hall.

"*The ice cream man! He's here! Please, Jerry, help! The ice cream man!*"

The voice belonged to Walter.

CHAPTER FIVE

"Let's go over this one more time, Walter. Omit no details."

Jerry sat on the arm of the couch next to Peter and folded his arms. An hour ago, at eight, they'd eaten breakfast in total silence but Peter knew they were all asking themselves the same question: *What had happened to Walter last night?* Peter'd only managed to munch a couple of slices of toast despite the English fry provided: bacon, eggs, sausages, beans, the works, but no salt. Not that it bothered him much; being clean still knotted his stomach. The smell had been enough to make Henry excuse himself twice, and Shelly Matthews still hadn't shown despite group therapy being underway.

Cold seeped inside the living room against the roaring fire's efforts, the window wet with condensation. The pulled-back curtains allowed in light that Peter avoided to sooth his tired eyes. He'd slept a little over three hours.

"I'd like to say something," Donald said. Peter noted the large man had managed to shave, looking fresher than the rest of the group. "That lady, Shelly? If she's gonna vomit every night, how am I expected to rest here? Walls are paper thin, Doc, heard the whole thing splash by splash."

Jerry nodded. "She's going through deep withdrawal, Donald, please understand. Heroin is difficult to kick."

"Sounded like she was dying, screaming her head off, for Christ's sake. Where is she? Ain't this shit mandatory?"

"She's in no state to join us today. Perhaps tomorrow."

Donald grunted a response and Jerry looked to the group. "Back to our discussion. Walter, please, go on."

"Jerry, look, I know he wasn't *really* there, okay? I just imagined it, I'm not stupid. I don't need to talk about it . . . I'm not crazy. It had just been frightening, you know? Really, really scared me."

"The reason to talk, Walter, is so that we can find the route of your problem, perhaps overcome it. An ice cream man is very specific. Sharing your thoughts with the group, somebody else might have had a similar experience and share theirs, too. Show you you're not alone."

Walter scratched his messed hair and pulled his bathrobe across him. "He'd seemed so *real*. Except for his jaw . . . That's why I peed myself. Geez, I'm so sorry about that. I peed the whole bed because his jaw reached all the way down to his stomach. It was so *long*! It . . . it waggled when he stepped, Jerry, back and forth, back and forth, all wet and red and shiny. I'm pretty sure he wanted to eat me."

"A nightmare, Walt. Last night before bed you told me last you knew this man. In real life. Would you mind sharing with the group?"

"The white uniform, the funny little hat . . . His shirt had WHIPPY'S written on the chest in blue letters. I know him from when I was a kid, you see. Me and my sister used to buy ice creams from him in the summer. My sister Annie, she's two years younger than me and she lives in Cincinnati now with her husband, and he doesn't like it when I call her so I don't do that anymore. But when we were kids, we'd buy ice creams off the ice cream man. He'd come in his truck once a day, every day, every summer. He was always so friendly, but he scared me because he spoke in a too-friendly voice that made me feel funny, and when he handed me my ice cream, or my change, his hand lingered on mine and it made me feel odd, like creepy crawlies make me feel. I'd felt sick when it happened, but I wanted to get my ice cream, you know? Come to think of it, I haven't had ice cream since. How strange is that? I've never thought about until you asked, but I've never eaten ice cream since I was a kid. And I loved that stuff."

"Do you think about that man often, Walter?"

"No!" Walter's eyes swelled behind their frames. "Never. I'd forgotten all about it until last night. It was him though, I know it. But his jaw was long and wiggling. I was trying to sleep and I felt nervous because usually my doctor gives me Zaleplon and it's my first night without those in months. They're sleeping tablets. Help me to go to sleep. My eyes wouldn't quit opening, and once when I opened them, he was just there, standing in the middle of the room. He looked just as I remembered but with that big, hanging jaw. I screamed and screamed and then the nice man with the beard opened the door and that made him disappear."

Jerry nodded. "Because he wasn't really there to begin with, right, Walter?"

"Right."

"Good."

Jerry made his way to a wooden armchair he'd set up at the top of the two couches and sat like a king on his throne. This morning he wore a thick black woolen sweater and looked more refreshed than anyone else in the room. "Does anyone have anything to add?"

Donald Bove arched an eyebrow and nodded towards Walter. "I'd like to say that he looks like shit."

"Donald, we're trying to be constructive here."

"Me, too. Nah, nah, don't get me wrong, I'm not pickin' on the guy. He just looks like shit."

"He's right," Jamie Peters said. "He does."

Peter had noticed, too, but he didn't want to be the one to say anything. Walter's face looked the texture of cheese. The whites of his eyes, magnified behind thick glasses, were streaked with veins and yellowed. Hair stood up at awkward angles around his head and he jittered, watching the group one by one.

"I don't feel so good," He said. "Like I caught a bug or something. My tummy doesn't feel right."

"That's antidepressant discontinuation syndrome, Walter," Jerry said. "It *will* pass, don't worry."

Walter tapped his temple. "I felt my brain zap me this morning, like an electric shock. *Zip.*"

"It's a common symptom for the syndrome, but I promise you it will pass. You might feel flu-ish and get a little dizziness over the next few days while your system clears itself but that's perfectly normal, too."

Donald leaned forward. "Hey, Walt, you say you never had no ice cream since you were a kid?"

"That's right."

"Well how's about you go get some ingredients, Fisher? My Momma, god bless her, used to make it homemade and I know how to make it just like her."

The gesture caught Peter off guard, coming from the big man it came across more like a threat. But then again, Peter imagined anything Donald said sounded like a threat.

"I don't know," Jerry said. "We'll think about it."

"S'the problem? You go to the town, or send one of the workin' fellas, pick some shit up. Boom, boom, done. I think Walt'd like that, eh?"

Walt nodded. "I would, Jerry, I would a lot."

Scratching at the bridge of his nose, Jerry sighed. "Let's see what I can do."

"Don't take no seein'? Don't take no nothin'." Donald stood and cupped his hands to his mouth. "Hey! Paul, Andy! You two out there?"

Jerry's face flashed red, only for a second, but enough for Peter to catch. "Donald. Do not disrupt this meeting."

"Ain't no problem, Fisher, all right?"

Andrew appeared at the living room door, wiping his hands in a cloth. "Yeah?"

"You," Donald said, pointing with each syllable. "If y'goin' inta town, I'd like you to pick me up some things, yeah?"

"Sure." Andrew nodded. "Not a problem."

Donald faced Jerry with a smirk. "See? Not a problem, Doc. Gonna make the man some lip-smackin' ice cream."

"Andrew," Jerry said. "Go back to your duties."

The group fell into an awkward silence as Andrew returned to the kitchen, then Jerry clapped his hands. "So, the first night was rough. Your bodies are adjusting to not getting what they want. It's a shock to the system. Withdrawals are awful, aren't they? But they'll get better with time, and we're all here to support one another in getting past that. Henry, you told us at the start of the meeting that alcohol was your vice. It's a hard habit to break. How did you feel last night?"

Henry watched Jerry with a steady gaze, looking both annoyed and ashamed at once. His voice came slow and steady. "I slept like shit, Jerry, if you must know. Usually by ten or eleven, I'd have had at least a bottle of something or other, numb and ready to pass out. Before I'd do that, a smoke or two helped me relax. My ritual, you could say. And I can't do that here."

"Smoke? Do you mean marijuana?"

"No. I haven't touched a joint since the seventies. Just tobacco. Without the nicotine, my head feels sick. I felt confused and anxious all night and I'm a little on edge this morning so forgive me if I say anything out of hand. I just might lose it at some point today. Know it's not intentional."

The last piece, Peter suspected, Henry meant for the group rather than Jerry Fisher.

"Do you usually have a problem with controlling your anger?" Jerry asked.

"Nope. Never an angry drunk, Jerry, nor abusive. Surprisingly, I'm more easy to agitate when I'm *not* drinking. The booze tames me, keeps me in check. Without it, and especially without a cigarette, I'm a little wound up, to say the least. Can't take the goddamn smokes off my mind for a second."

"The work today will help with that. You'll find yourself focusing on the tasks at hand, and the fresh air will work wonders. I guarantee it." Jerry looked to the young man seated next to Henry like a lion looks to prey, and Jamie Peters eyed the room, looking anywhere else. The young man's hair clung to his forehead and he rubbed his hands together.

"Jamie," Jerry said. "How was your night?"

Jamie flashed a smile. His voice sounded slurred, but Peter guessed that to be his natural voice. "S'all right."

"Okay. And how are you *feeling*?"

"I'm feeling pretty low, if m'honest. Feel depressed."

"Abuse of prescription drugs will do that. Your mom said she found a stash of hydrocodone in your room, and those *pharming* parties nearly killed your friend Liam from what I hear. You know they're opiates, don't you? In the same family as heroin, right?"

"I know."

"Okay. Well, the withdrawal period will start, and when it does, you'll be working with Andrew, who you've already met. I think you'll get through it. We'll work on our one-to-one counseling in private and make sure to set a relapse-prevention program into place. Stop you from cracking up."

Peter's stomach lurched. "Jerry, that's a little uncalled for?"

Ignoring the comment, the doctor smirked. "Sick stomach, the shakes, it'll happen, but if you're strong enough, you'll survive . . . Donald. Your night?"

Looking to the kid, Peter felt a moment of pity. He'd judged him yesterday, lumping him into the same group of jocks Peter'd known as a teenager. But Jamie wasn't a jock in this room; here he was a junkie who needed help as bad as the rest of them. One who didn't deserve to be bullied by the likes of Jerry Fisher.

Non-judgmental team my ass, Peter thought.

Then Donald cleared his throat. Peter expected another sly remark from the man but instead, he pushed his palms into his eyes and blew out a breath. "Doc, it's bad. It's real bad. Not having a bump, y'know? It's making me anksy. Feelin' anksy. No blow, man, never thought the day would come. You know, you go into a new area and you need a bump, you suss the joint by seeing who's sniffling. That tweaky sniffler's your guy, y'know? *That's* the guy. And I'm still thinkin' that way. Looking around here at all you, wondering who's got some blow. Wonderin' who's my guy."

"You're talking about cocaine?"

"Do I look like a gear-head, Doc? I'm a fiend, yeah, I'll admit it. Look at me, for crying out loud, can hardly sit still here. Crack started comin' in around eighty-four where I'm from, but I never touched the shit. Well, briefly, but only because they used to sell it on Selma and Orange and I had no other choice, know what I'm sayin'? But coke's my thing, yeah. Just having that package man, having that package. *Completes* you. Right now, I don't feel complete 'cause I don't got my package."

"Your emotions will be high while we detox, Donald. And a good diet is going to help. The work will keep you busy. We'll talk more in our private sessions, all right?"

Jerry's sympathy caused Peter to frown. Only a moment ago, the doctor had picked on Jamie Peters . . . Was he trying to weasel back into the group's good book? Or else, and this frightened Peter, had he *imagined* the dig at Jamie? Was he getting paranoid?

"All right, Doc," Donald said. "You the boss, man."

"Okay then." Now Jerry turned his attention to Peter, making something flutter inside him. His heart raced as each eye in the room watched on. He wanted to sink through the floorboards, sink down and be anywhere else but here. Shit, if he never would have come here he could be outside enjoying the frosty morning, flushing out his system alone. Jogging. That could've helped. Why didn't he try jogging before blowing nearly two grand on this shit? Some smoothies, drink more water . . .

"Mister Laughlin? Your first night. Do you have anything to say?"

"Fine and dandy, Doc. Slept like a baby."

At once, both Donald and Jamie gave a cold stare, but not Henry. Peter could tell the old man knew it to be a bluff by the slight smile playing on his lips. The other two might think of him as the lucky one, gliding through the program while they struggled at the bottom, but there'd be time to get them alone and talk; see if they caught Fisher's bad attitude, too.

A sound came from the kitchen, a sharp bang followed by a meow. The group turned as one as a black and white cat sauntered into the room with its tail batting back and forth. It gave a light purr before easing itself into a sitting position.

"I hope none of you have allergies," Jerry said. "I should have asked ahead but this is quite a surprise, we haven't seen Alisa in a week so I'd assumed she'd left us for a better home. I can't tell you how happy I was when we pulled up yesterday and there she was, snoozing on the porch."

Donald looked from the cat to Jerry and back again. "A cat, Doc? We got a cat? I haven't had one of those since I was a kid. Named it Joey, that's what I did. Found it out in the yard one night, think somebody dumped the poor fuck. Yeah, forgot all about that little guy. Momma let me keep it, can you believe that?"

"You're more than welcome to feed her if you'd like, Donald. There's leftovers from breakfast I'm sure she'd appreciate."

"Yeah? For real?" Donald shifted his large frame from the couch. "Yeah, I'd like that." His expression softened in a way Peter didn't think possible. "I do it now? That good?"

"Sure. Paul is still cleaning up in the kitchen, ask him if you need anything. Also, there's a stable out the back where Alisa is used to sleeping. The horses are long gone, Harris sold them when he renovated the place, but now that Alisa is back we could use someone to make it cozy for her. Clean it up and get a bed set. That can be your first job."

"Sure thing, man. I can do that."

Jerry looked to the group. "The rest of you, please follow me into the yard to get the day started."

The morning frost bit at Peter's cheeks. He'd gone to his room and collected his leather jacket before joining the others outside. He hadn't worn the jacket in years, but it still fit good and felt great. Gloves and a scarf protected his hands and neck, a set he'd bought in the shopping center while waiting for the rest of the guests to arrive the morning before. As he followed the rest of the group, lazy snowflakes drifted down, sticking to the mud and grass before dissolving.

Henry squinted at the sky. "Looks like it's going to get pretty heavy soon, don't you think?"

"Yes," Jerry agreed. "But it won't stick. Nothing to worry about. Never seems to stick around these parts, especially when the sun is still out. Still, I better get Andrew to go to down to town and pick up some supplies before the roads get too icy."

"We need to get Walter his ingredients for that ice cream at the very least," Henry said. He smiled at Walter. "Don't we?"

Walter walked in circles, flapping his arms against his thick sports coat and making a puffing sound. "Yes please, I'd like that," he said, watching the flakes dance down with child-like fascination.

Jerry cleared his throat. "Amongst other things. In the meantime, Peter, see our barn?" He pointed to the large outbuilding on the right, sitting atop a hill. Red-painted planks looked faded from time, the white double doors now a dirty cream.

"A good bit of the timber got moldy from the weather. We need to replace them as soon as possible and I've got some new planks ready inside. If you spot any degraded planks, simply remove them and slot in a new one with the tools I've provided. We'll need to stain them afterward, but we'll take it one step at a time for now. Have you ever done anything like it before?"

"Yes. My girl—" Peter paused before saying *girlfriend*. "My *friend*'s father used to have a barn next door to my grandmother's place. Helped him do it up one summer after it got rot in the winter."

"Good, then you've done this very thing. Jamie, would you mind helping Peter?"

The young man nodded.

"Okay then, get to it. The rest of you follow me."

Peter left the group and made for the barn, Jamie trudging behind with his hands in his pockets. He wanted to make conversation with the kid, ask him what he thought of Fisher, but he found it hard to find the right words. He'd never met someone with an addiction to prescription drugs before, but once, on tour, the lead singer of a headlining act had taken Xanax nearly every night. Then again, that guy took just about anything he could get his hands on. Peter wouldn't have called it the man's *vice*.

"Hopefully the work will warm us up a bit, huh?" He said.

Jamie didn't respond. Instead, he wiped his nose, which had grown red in the cold. Their boot heels crunched the frozen grass as they slogged uphill.

"You ever do anything like this before?"

Jamie stopped. "Look man, I don't need this bullshit."

Peter's stomach lurched. He turned and faced the kid. "I'm sorry?"

"I don't need to talk to you. I don't need to talk to anyone, got it? I'm getting through this m'self."

"All right, kid," Peter said with a chuckle. "Take it easy."

"Take it easy? You're telling me to take it easy?" Jamie's hands curled into tight fists. "You're a fucking *loser*, man. You *all* are. I'm here to get through this m'self. Don't need you telling me what to do."

"Hey, no need for that, all right?"

"What's going on here?" Henry's voice came from downhill as the old man trudged towards them. Peter hoped he wouldn't have a heart attack. "What's the problem?"

Peter shouted back. "No problem, Henry. We're all good here."

And that's when the punch hit.

CHAPTER SIX

The world exploded a sea of black and red. Peter gasped and held his nose, losing grip on the frozen ground. He blinked, watching as stars danced across his vision. The pain in his nose swelled.

"Hey, hey! Stop that!"

Henry grappled Jamie's arm, wrestling it down before shoving the youth in the chest. Jamie stumbled back, regaining his footing and looking like a bull ready to charge.

Henry shook his head. "What the hell is wrong with you, kid? That's no way to act here."

Jamie didn't answer. Instead, he stared at them both, his nostrils flaring. He clenched his fists. "I got a girl at home, a football team that needs me back by the start of season, I'm not like you losers. I've got a *life*."

Peter dabbed at his nose, wincing at the zap of pain. "Shit. Nose is bleeding."

His glove came away glistening as he sniffled back a warm flow. The metallic taste of blood filled the back of his throat. "Shit."

"What's going on here?"

As Jerry Fisher made his way up the hill, his breath streamed away in clouds. He jogged to the three of them. "What's happened, huh?"

Peter motioned to Jamie. "Guy bopped me in the face." His voice sounded funny from squeezing at the bridge of his nose. He felt embarrassed, but good, too, for not entertaining the idea of a fight. Especially not with someone so young. "He clipped me in the nose, now it's bleeding. That's what happened."

"Jamie, come with me," Jerry said. "Peter, will you be all right?"

"Dandy, Doc. Just dandy."

As Jerry lead Jamie down to the farmhouse, he mumbled to the youth and put an arm around his shoulders. When they'd gone, Peter looked to Henry. "Can you believe that shit?"

"Kid just cracked you one?"

"Yeah, I just asked if he'd ever done any work like this before. Was trying to make conversation, you know?"

"It's all right. Take it easy." Henry led him to a nearby tree and lowered Peter's hands from his face. He studied the blow, his head moving side to side. Peter smelled coffee on his breath. "Looks all right, doesn't look broken to me, at least. Hurt?"

"Yeah, hurts. Throbbing. More embarrassing than anything."

"No, embarrassing would be trying to explain to everybody why you beat up a teenager. Good thing you didn't fight back, at least in this case."

"Suppose you're right."

Peter sniffed back another gush of blood, feeling as if a tap had been turned on inside his head. Nausea swam in his stomach.

"You know," Henry said. "My folks used to tell me never to tilt my head back when I got a nosebleed. Said it would go inside my stomach and turn me sick. I don't know if that's true or not, but I do think we should get you down to the house and have you cleaned up. You good with that?"

"Yeah, that sounds like a plan."

Henry clapped Peter on the back. "Good. Come on."

As they made their way downhill, blood dripped from Peter's right nostril. He dabbed it with his glove. *Perfect*, He thought. *My new fucking gloves.*

He looked to Henry. "Cocky little brat, isn't he?"

Henry laughed, shaking his head. "Damn right about that. Who do you think paid for him to be here?"

"Said he had a football team that needs him. From the sounds of it, I'd think a joint finance between the school and his parents. By the looks of him, by the fact Jerry said he hosted *pharming* parties, I'm guessing his parents are rich. One of 'em is probably a doctor. How else would he get all that medication?"

"What are *pharming* parties?"

"Ah, kids fish around inside their bathroom cupboards, find prescription medications and the like, go to somebody's house and put 'em in a big bowl. Like playing Russian Roulette with candies. Except the outcome is much different."

Shaking his head, Henry asked, "Are they completely idiotic?"

Peter laughed, breathing through his mouth. "I know, right? But like we're the ones to speak."

Henry climbed the porch steps and held the door open. "Here."

"Thanks."

They made their way to the kitchen, Peter's eyes trained on the wall to keep his head held in one position. He passed a framed, black and white photograph of a family and paused. In the picture, a couple smiled with a baby cradled between them.

"Dawson's family?"

"Huh?"

Peter nodded to the photograph. "There. His parents, I'd assume?"

"Most likely. I saw the gun rack first, though, if I'm honest."

"Jesus."

At the head of the hall stood a mahogany cabinet, a fat lock lying against its doors. "Good thing it's sealed," Peter said. "What with us crazies drying out and all."

"Very funny. Come on."

Henry led him into the dining-room and told him to wait while he went to the kitchen and Peter thanked him. He pushed his back against the wall and took a deep breath, the smell of fresh vegetables and coffee hitting his throbbing nose. Somewhere in the next room, a radio played what his grandmother liked to call *elevator music*. She'd always been a country music fan herself. Henry returned.

"Here, move your hands."

Something cold and wet pressed against his face. Peter took the damp cloth in both of his hands and sniffled, snorting some water in the process. "Thanks, man. I really appreciate it."

"Don't worry about it. You feeling all right?"

"Yeah, I'm good." Peter dabbed his nose. "You know, something Jerry said earlier that bothered me. You notice it?"

"How he handled Jamie?"

"Yeah."

"Yeah, I noticed." Henry folded his arms. "Not saying anything this early, but if that kind of carry-on continues, I'm out of here. I didn't like how he handled Walter, either."

"How do you mean?"

"I mean, if he's a trained psychologist and counselor, he should have taken Walter aside, one on one, you know? Not say it out loud in front of everyone. Didn't come across as very professional to me, felt more like poking fun at the fat kid."

"You think he's a hack? Jerry?"

"I'm just saying what I'm thinking. I mean, for two grand, and it wasn't easy for me to scrape that together let me tell you, you'd think there'd be . . . I don't know, a little *more* to this? Did you research Jerry Fisher? Or Harris Dawson?"

"Don't scare me, dude. I didn't think I'd need to, took his word for it. I spoke to him on the phone."

"Me, too. I'm just worried everyone else did the same thing and we're all being scammed here."

"But if it's a scam, what purpose would it serve? Because once we're out and know they're frauds, we could easily report it and bring them to court. Seems like a lot of work for a bad scam."

Henry's face fell. "Maybe. But I just had a bad feeling ever since we arrived. Call it intuition." He leaned forward and lowered his voice. "I tell you what, see how he handles you on your one-to-one sessions. I'll do the same. Could you do that?"

"I will."

Henry grabbed Peter's wrist. Not hard, but firm. "I know I'm probably just being paranoid here, and most likely you don't believe my gut, but humor me with this one. Please."

The sincerity in the old man's voice made Peter sad. Were they a couple of paranoid drunks who believed the world was out to get them? If so, it could lead to a mess break down in counselling for either one of them, but at least the plan was something to do. They'd need something more to work with besides Jerry's jab at Jamie.

"I'll do it. When I have my session, I'll pay very close attention. In the meantime, I have another idea." Peter dabbed at his nose and looked to the cloth. The bleeding had slowed. "Follow me."

Peter crossed the room to the green swing door and shouldered it open, intensifying the smell of coffee and the noise of the radio. In the kitchen, Paul hummed to himself, flattening out a pastry base on the countertop. He threw them a smile before continuing with his work.

"Howdy, fellas."

"Hey, Paul. Compliments to the chef for the breakfast."

Paul smiled a perfectly white and straight set of teeth. "Thank you. I do appreciate that. Lot of leftovers from you guys, lot of leftovers, but at least you enjoyed what you ate. It's nice to cook with gas again, I can tell you that. Back home we got electric ovens but I always preferred the taste of something grilled on a gas cooker, know what I'm saying? That's a real cook, right there." He rapped his knuckles on two propane canisters beneath the table. "That's the real deal."

"Sure." Peter rinsed his cloth in a nearby sink and watched the water turn a light pink. He waited for it to run clear. "Hey, Paul, how long have you worked here? Couple of years now?"

"Oh, no, nothing like that." Paul stopped rolling his pasty and folded his arms. "It's Monday, right? So, just going on seven days, I believe."

"Ah. And Andrew? He's been here a long time?"

"Nope. Andrew and I signed on the same time. Seems staff rotation around here is commonplace, being there's only two weeks' work every few months, know what I'm saying?"

"Sure, sure. And you're a trained counselor, right?"

"Me?" Paul laughed, his face turning to mock shock. "Me, a counselor, like Mr. Fisher? Lord, no. Been a chef since I finished college. Damn fine one at that, if I might add. A little scared of working night shift taking care of you folk but I'll do all right, don't you worry. Not like you're insane or anything." Paul's smile disappeared. "I'm sorry, that was a little insensitive of me."

Peter laughed. "Not to worry, man. Sorry for the confusion. Anyway, we'll leave you to it. Have a nice day."

"Yeah, you too, man."

The radio muted as the door swung shut again. In the dining room, Peter turned to Henry, the old man looking confused.

"What was that all about? That guy Paul's just a chef but he's working as a nighttime caretaker to us, too? That illegal?"

"I'd say at the very least it's poor practice. Not something you'd expect from a grand-a-week deal."

"Why would Jerry do that?"

"I don't know, man. If it's all a scam, then to cut back on costs, maybe? Cheaper to hire a chef and security guy than to hire two trained counselors who can cook and night watch."

"I'm sure. But Paul seemed genuinely shocked when you asked him if he was a counselor, and if he'd known about the scam, there'd been some giveaway on his face. I'm sure Paul and Andrew are just as out of the loop as the rest of us. We need to confront Jerry about this. I am not being made a fool of."

"Yeah," Peter agreed, reaching out to stop Henry. "But let's do our one-on-one sessions first, all right? We could just be jumping the gun here. Maybe we're suspicious over nothing. A wrong phrase, a cutback on staff that overall, is understandable, if they're not actually counseling us but cooking and night watching. Could just be something Jerry said to make the guests feel more comfortable, you know? Give it a little time."

"Okay." Henry looked ashamed, his eyes glistening. "Am I just embarrassing myself, kid? Am I really that cynical of everybody?"

"No, of course not. Hey man, I'm suspicious, too. I just don't want to jump the gun with it, that's all. Something will either confirm it for us, or deny it. Let's wait for that."

"If you say so." Henry looked him in the eye. "Strange phrase you use. Jump the gun. I've only ever heard jumped the shark, myself."

Peter smiled. "It's my grandmother. She's full of those. A rolling stone gathers no moss, that was another. Early to bed, early to rise. She's like a one-liner jukebox."

"You miss her?"

"Of course." Peter's chest lurched. "She's my only family now, after my mom died. Dad was never in the picture to begin with. Lived on a small farm, just outside of the city. Such a strong lady. Raised me alone after my mom and grandfather both passed, but never let it get her down. I'm sure inside she was falling apart, but she was strong for both of us, and I had a happy childhood. I just want to make her proud now. Be strong for her this time, return the favor. Maybe do something good for her for once, when we get out. One of the main reasons I'm here. That, and something else. But I don't want to talk about it."

Henry smiled, taking a decade off his face. "You're a good kid, Peter. Come on, I'll help you with the barn. I'm sure you'll have your session with Fisher soon."

They walked to the barn in silence and began their work. Henry commented that the falling snow seemed to be sticking, contrary to what Jerry Fisher had said. Piles of white powder lay cluttered in the grass and weighed down the trees in the forest. Peter agreed it didn't seem to be going anywhere. The temperature had dropped, too—not a whole lot, but noticeable.

They removed a total of fifteen rotting planks from the left wall of the barn, extracting the rusted nails with the back of a hammer like decayed teeth. They stocked the dead planks in a pile and nailed in the healthy replacements. Peter found the smell of fresh wood soothing. He hadn't smelled it in a long time, and it worked wonders on his mind, rinsing out the adrenaline of earlier events.

Working with his hands felt good, too. The new planks were heavy, and it felt productive just to hold them. It felt important. The fresh cut of the wood left splinters tacked to his new gloves, but he didn't mind; they were soaked in nose blood, anyway. The dull throbbing in his nose had even subsided.

They worked that way for an hour before Peter paused and chuckled.

"Something funny, kid?"

"Yeah, actually . . ." Peter shook his head. "This is the first time I can remember not needing a cigarette. Sorry, *wanting* a cigarette, I should say."

"Here's to the working men."

"Hear, hear."

Then Jerry Fisher knocked on the barn door.

"Sorry to disturb you, fellas."

The counselor's stubbled cheeks lifted in a smile. He wore a black scarf over his polo neck, and melting snowflakes stuck to his shoulders and hair. A waft of aftershave drifted from him, tainting the honest smell of raw wood. "Peter, I was hoping we might start our one-to-one session soon, does that sound all right?"

Removing his gloves, Peter wiped the sweat on his forehead. "Sure, Jerry. Sounds good."

"Any troubles with the barn? Looks like you fellas know what you're doing."

Henry leaned on the dead pile of planks and raised his palm. "All good, Jerry. No problems here."

"Excellent. Peter? Would you like to follow me?"

"Sure thing."

He gave Henry a wink as he left, causing the old man to snort a laugh. *See ya later, buddy*, Peter thought. *At least our little game will pass the time.*

Peter jogged and caught up to Fisher, his toes numb in his boots. The sound of a brush sweeping echoed from the stable behind the farmhouse.

"Mr. Bove's doing a fine job," Jerry said, his breath drifting away in a mist-like pillar. "That stable's going to be a nice place for Alisa. I'm sure she'll be very pleased not having to share it with any horses. Walter is replacing some of the rotted boards in there, too, just like you're doing to the barn."

"Oh? Walter's out working?"

"Yes. He'd be no good to anyone cooped up inside the house."

Sure, Peter thought. *Best give him a hammer and let him roam free.*

"Snow looks like it might stick after all, what do you think?"

"It might," Jerry said. "But even if it does get heavy, we have our supplies. Andrew just arrived back from town. We'll be okay."

Jerry gave a quick smile and Peter returned it, all the while thinking: *But you said it wouldn't stick . . . That's two, Fisher.*

Peter cleared his throat. "Hey, did Andrew get Walter's ice cream ingredients?"

Jerry's face twitched. They reached the farmhouse. "After you."

"Right."

Grocery bags greeted Peter as he entered the house. He sidestepped them and scanned their contents; fruit, vegetables, packets of cooked ham, frozen chicken, cheese, bottled water, dozens of eggs, and . . .

"Hey, look, Walter's ice cream stuff."

Jerry stopped as if someone had slapped his face. He spun and eyed the bags, his breath coming in tight bursts.

Worry slithered across Peter like a cold snake. "Everything all right, Jerry?"

"Sure, Peter. Everything is fine. Fine."

Jerry's eyes stayed on the bags and Peter looked between them and him. "Jerry, it's just some ice cream, no need to get so worked up, right? If I'm honest, Walter doesn't seem all too well after his ordeal last night. I think he's earned this, don't you?"

"Sure. Yes. He has . . . Follow me, Peter."

"Okay . . ."

Peter took one last look at the bag. FOR WALTER marked the paper in black ink. A liter of milk sat inside, along with a bag of sugar, a carton of eggs, cream, a container of rock salt, and vanilla extract.

Lip-smackin', Peter thought. *Lip-smackin' ice cream.*

"In here. My office."

Jerry held the door open as Peter stepped inside. Two comfortable-looking brown leather armchairs sat facing each other in the middle of the room, taking up most the tight space. Through the single window ahead, Peter saw the barn on top of the hill as snowflakes danced past the glass. A tall lamp cast a soft glow from the corner of the room, the scent of pine pervading the air.

"Peter, have a seat."

As Jerry closed the door, Peter lowered himself into one of the armchairs, the leather groaning and contouring to his body. Jerry sat in the chair opposite chair, scanning a notebook on the armrest.

"I do apologize for Jamie's behavior earlier. Coming off prescription medication can have a myriad of effects on the mind. He's anxious. His emotions are running high. Is your nose all right?"

"It's fine, man. Not to worry." The dull throbbing had lessened over the course of the last hour, and Peter thought it would be gone soon enough. "I understand where he's coming from, lashing out as a young man. We've all been there. No hard feelings."

"Yes, well, I finished talking to him before I came and got you. He's very apologetic. I made him promise that it won't happen again." Jerry laced his fingers together. "So, Peter, anything on your mind?"

Peter's mouth went dry. He hadn't prepared for any of this. If conversation turned to Beth, or alcohol, he didn't know how he'd respond. Goddamn, he wanted a cigarette.

"What's on my mind, Jerry, is Walter. The guy didn't look too well this morning. At all. I know we're all flushing out our systems, we're not going to be in the best of shape, but there was something more to Walter. His eyes. His skin . . . Jesus."

"Walter's a weak man. It hit him first."

"*It?*" Peter sat forward. "What hit him first?"

"The pressure of this detox, Peter, there's no need to be so defensive. We're not out to get you."

"Who do you mean *we?*"

Jerry shook his head and grinned. "Myself and doctor Dawson, of course, Peter. Relax. I'm here to help."

Relaxing was the last thing on Peter's mind; his heart jackhammered his chest and his palms were sweaty. The room felt too small. "How are you going to handle Walter? Are you qualified to deal with his kind of behavior? You gave him a hammer."

Jerry's smile twitched at the sides, as if he found it hard to keep in place. "We're keeping a close eye on him to make sure he's safe and continues to get healthy. Walter is not your concern."

Anger boiled inside Peter. It felt like Jerry was *handling* him. "I don't know why you were so against the ice cream plan, but I think Walt's deserved it, don't you?"

Jerry nodded, his smile still struggling to stay afloat.

"I get the feeling you don't like me very much, Fisher."

Jerry's brow creased. "Now, Peter, what an awful thing to say.

We're getting off on the wrong foot here."

Peter leaned forward, his arms shaking with adrenaline. "You know what my grandmother says, Jerry? She says when somebody lies, they can't look you in the eye. Anyone with even a basic *interest* in psychology or human nature would know that. And if you knew that, you'd have done it. Why didn't you look me in the eye right now, Jerry?"

Jerry shook his head with a sigh. "You're getting hostile, Peter. I'm not your enemy. What I want to know is how you *feel*. You mentioned your grandmother. She's a very nice lady. Do you want to talk about your relationship?"

Peter's stomach dropped. "How do you know about my grandmother?"

"From Harris Dawson, of course. We do a background check on each of our guests so I can have a foundation for our talks. It's part of the procedure."

"We're not talking about my grandmother."

He saw something in Jerry's eyes just then, something *knowing*. "I'm not going to force you to talk, but you have to be willing to drop your defensive attitude soon. When you do, I'll be here to listen to you . . . Good day, Laughlin."

"That's it? We're done here?"

"We're done. Until you're willing to open up, there's nothing more I can do. Why don't you finish your work with Mr. Randolph on the barn until dinner is ready?"

Peter shook his head and rose from the chair. He didn't spare another glance in Jerry Fisher's direction as he left the room. His skin crawled as the door creaked shut and he felt Jerry's eyes on his back. He shivered. Something'd happened in there.

He walked quickly through the house, his boots thumping on the hardwood, and made his way to the barn. The cold air hit his too-hot skin and he realized he'd been sweating.

Paranoia? He thought. *Is that what happened? Maybe what's wrong is the fact that once you pull the top off everything that's bottled up—you don't know how much shit's going to come spewing out. And what's worse is you don't know if you'll be able to control it. Henry's the same . . . He's just like you. You're both afraid to bring what's deep inside your rotting minds to the surface, because it's been down there for a long time, festering and fermenting . . . Who knows what might happen if you open up?*

"Peter, are you all right?" Henry stood at the barn door, his face red from labor. "How did it go?"

Peter sighed and looked about the yard. A pair of rooks took flight from a tree in the forest, disappearing into the snow. "I don't know," he said.

"You don't know how it went, or you don't know if you're okay?"

"Both."

Peter looked into the old man's eyes, hating how conflicted his emotions were. "I don't know if Jerry is doing something wrong, or if I'm just afraid to open up. Whichever it is, it doesn't change the outcome. Either one seems sad."

"Sit down, take a breather. Come on."

Henry led him inside to the dead wood pile where another three planks had been added. Dust floated in the air.

"We're going to be tweaky and unsettled for a while," Henry said. "That's for sure. But I think Jerry's up to something. I don't think we should let this lie."

"Stop, Henry."

Peter clasped his neck and paced the room. He needed a cigarette, bad.

"Go to Fisher and do your session. I gave him shit when I don't think I should have."

"You think this is all legit?"

Peter sat on the deadwood. "I think we're frightened. And I think that's normal. Go to your session, Henry. Open up to Fisher. I think you need to. And I think that I do, too."

Henry went to the barn wall without a word and began working, smacking nails into a fresh plank with a little more force than Peter thought necessary.

"Hey, Henry, don't be—"

"Don't tell me what to do or be, Peter, understand?"

The old man's eyes widened, his breathing heavy. After a tense moment, he went back to hammering. Peter picked up a nearby plank and went to work, too.

CHAPTER SEVEN

"It was him, I saw him!"

Peter jolted awake at the sound of the voice. He sat upright, his heart thumping.

Henry?

The old man sounded drunk.

Throwing off his sweaty blanket, Peter peered at the digital alarm clock by the bed, the light stinging his eyes. Three in the morning; he'd only been out half an hour.

The noise of running feet came from outside the room, two sets of feet by the sounds of it, then a thump. It sounded as if Henry had fallen out of his bed.

Peter pulled on his pajamas and took the room in two strides, his head heavy with sleep. He squinted against the light in the hallway, spotting Jerry Fisher and the caretaker, Andrew, standing in Henry's doorway. He made his way over to them.

"What's going on?" He asked. "What's happening?"

"Go back to your room," Jerry said. He stood in Henry's doorway, blocking the room. "We'll handle this. Go back to sleep."

Peter craned his neck to see over Fisher's shoulder into the room. On the floor lay Henry, looking like a discarded doll.

"Holy shit, what's happened?"

The old man sat pressed against the wall, his face glistening in the glow of the hall light. A trail of spit leaked from his lower lip as he mewled like an injured animal, his face scrunched in pain.

Frustration overcame Peter. "Jerry! Let me see what's happening, goddamn it."

"We don't know what's happening just yet, Laughlin. *Go back to bed.*"

"Fuck this."

Peter barged into the room, elbowing Jerry aside. He heard

the other guests in the hallway now, their voices full of sleep and confusion.

Peter got to his knees and put a hand on Henry's shoulder. "Henry? Henry? You all right? Can you speak?"

"He was here, he was . . ." Henry's voice came out a single slur, sounding five bottles beyond sober. "He crawled, just like he'd been learnin' . . . All over my bed."

Henry's head hit the wall with a sickening thump and Peter stood, backing away in shock. His heart smacked his ribcage.

Jerry motioned to Andrew. "We need to get him down to the living room. Help me get him up."

Together, they hoisted the old man to his feet, draping his arms around their shoulders. Henry's eyes shot open.

"Off of me! The fuck offa me!"

The old man wrestled himself free, his legs working against each other and sending him smacking against the wall. He righted himself and swayed. "He was here, s'all true. M'boy was here."

"Henry . . ." Peter stepped forward and licked at his lips. "It's me. Peter. You feeling all right?"

"C'mere." Henry motioned with a wave of his hand, a sick grin sliding onto his lips. "Am I feelin' all right? S'that what you asking, yeah?"

"Yes." Peter's stomach cartwheeled, the old man's stare burning into him. Somewhere in the room, he guessed hidden bottles lay empty. Henry looked drunk as a skunk. "Henry, I'm just trying—"

The punch connected.

For the second time in less than twenty-four hours, Peter's vision exploded into bright lights. He stumbled back, hitting the wall as Jerry and Andrew struggled to restrain the old man. Henry shouted an unintelligible string of slurs, his body flailing against the two men. Then he fell silent.

Peter opened his eyes, his hand pressed to his stinging cheek. Unlike Jamie Peters, Henry had calloused working hands, and those dry, hard knuckles had imprinted just below his right eye. A deep stinging began to inflate, the chunk of flesh throbbing as the taste of copper filled his mouth. Quite simply, it hurt like a bitch.

"Move, move."

Jerry and Andrew pushed past with Henry lolling between them, his feet lax and dragging on the floor. They rushed to the staircase, taking no time to answer questions from the guests. Peter stumbled into the hallway after.

"Hey," Donald said, knotting the belt of his silk bathrobe. "The fuck happened in there, kid? Huh?"

"I don't know."

Down the corridor, Shelly Matthews screamed, shredding her vocal chords.

"Jesus fuckin' Christ!" Donald said. "The fuck is goin' on tonight?"

"She must have woke up from the racket," Walter said from the other side of the hall. He looked nervous, his complexion pale. "Should someone check on her? Jerry and Andrew are downstairs, it's gotta be one of us."

Fuck, Peter thought. *This is just great.*

From downstairs came the sound of a door opening, followed by the two men's footsteps. Then the door closed, leaving the house in silence. Shelly Matthews whimpered, the sound muted from her room. Peter looked to the others, and they looked to him.

Walter, wearing a navy blue night robe, hugged himself, while Donny looked more confused than frightened, squeezing his fists together in an almost calculated fashion. Jamie Peters leaned on his doorframe, his face unreadable. Peter had the impression the three of them were waiting for him to do something.

"Pete," Donald said, breaking the silence. "You know, you wanna go check on her, I'd say nothin'. Sounds like she's in bad shape down there. Walt's right, one of us gotta do something."

"No, no, *no*." Walter shook his head. "I changed my mind. If Jerry finds out he'll be furious. Let's just go back to bed."

"Okay then," Donald agreed. "Walter, go back to bed. We'll all do the same."

"Thank you, Mr. Bove. Goodnight, everyone."

Walter returned to his room, the door clicking shut behind

him. The others waited a moment, Shelly Matthews' whimpering hanging in the air. Donald's eyes stayed locked on Peter.

"Go on," he said. "I know you wanna. I ain't gonna say a word. Not one. She sounds in pain." He nodded to Jamie, his eyebrow arched. "Kid? Gonna say a word?"

Jamie shook his head, eyes down.

"Good. Then get back to bed 'cause you didn't see nothin'."

Jamie returned to his room, leaving the two men. Donald cocked a thumb in the direction of Shelly's room. "Want me to hold your fuckin' hand or somethin'? Go check on the chick."

Why don't you check on her if you're so concerned, big man? Peter thought. He knew better than to pick a fight with someone like Donald. *Still, all talk . . .*

Despite his conflicting inner ramblings, Peter heard himself say, "Okay. I'll go." His throat had turned to sandpaper.

He made his way down the hall, his heart trying to escape his chest. Donald stayed at his bedroom door, arms folded and watching like a gargoyle. Licking at his lips, Peter continued.

He'd never dealt with a heroin addict before. What would be inside the room? The smell of shit and piss, maybe; that was high probability. Puke, too. She'd most likely be slicked with sweat, her eyes bulging from their sockets, shaking and scared senseless. But Peter worried she might need water, *something,* and that's what kept his legs moving. He couldn't leave her unattended to marinate in her own juices, he'd want somebody to do the same for him.

Just because you pretend a problem isn't there doesn't mean it's not. Another great line from Granny. One that always came back to him in times of trouble, and one that applied to the current situation. Peter reached for the door handle and took a deep breath, readying himself for the horror within. He opened the door and found—

Nothing. An empty room.

The fresh bed sat unoccupied, the curtains drawn. A dresser gathered dust in the corner next to a laundry shoot and a reading lamp. The place didn't smell of shit, piss, or even vomit. In fact, the room smelt *fresh,* like pine air freshener. No signs of Shelly Matthews ever being in the room existed. Peter's voice sounded as if it come from down a well to his own ears. "Donald." He said. "Come here, please."

The big man approached and stood behind him in the doorway. "The fuck's goin' on here?" he said, his voice a whisper. "We *definitely* heard her, right? In this room?"

"Right."

"Then what the fuck's happening?"

They examined the room, Peter getting to his knees and scanning beneath the bed. "I don't know what to say, Donald . . ."

"Donny. Ain't nobody call me Donald 'cept for my mother. Listen, I'm tweakin' out. I ain't gone this long without a bump since the Daddy Bush era. So, tell me, kid, she ain't here, but we heard her. That correct?"

"Yeah. I heard her. Definitely."

"And you ain't no junkie freak or nothin', right? Alcoholic or somethin'?"

"Or something. I heard her, too, don't worry."

"Bed's made, no baggage, place clean as a bell . . ."

Peter had no response.

"Let's get out of here," Donald said.

Peter closed the door over without a sound, trying not to attract the attention of Fisher or one of the orderlies. He didn't know which of the staff members he could trust, if any.

"Hey," Donald said. "Somethin' fishy's goin' on here. You know that, I can see it in your eyes. The kid? What's his name, James? Jamie? He don't know shit. Just keeping his head down. And that Walter guy? You could put a snake in his room and he probably wouldn't find it outta line. But you, you and the old man? You got a sense of what I'm talkin' about. I know a liar when I sees one, and that Jerry Fisher fella, I tell you, *he's one big fat fuckin' liar*." The word came out *liah* from the big man's mouth, but Peter got the message.

"Donny, Henry and I came up with something. Well, Henry did. He doesn't trust Jerry either. Now, with this Shelly girl gone? I agree, man, something's up. Henry wants to keep an eye on Jerry for signs of, I don't know, *something*. And I have a feeling we're going to see that something soon enough."

"Hey," Donald said. "You and the old man got somethin' goin', I want in. And I gotta ask you, you think the old man found some booze? Stashed it? I seen the way he was, kid, and if that ain't a boozer then I ain't fat."

"He paid two thousand dollars to be here, and from the man I got to know, I don't think so."

"How's that?"

"I don't know yet."

Peter didn't, but to take a page from Henry's way of thought, *call it instinct*. Some event clearly haunted the old man, but Peter hoped the hook wasn't too deep that even Henry, who appeared dedicated to getting clean, would lie to fall off the wagon and lie in the gutter. Despite taking a punch from him, Peter still had hope for the old man. Even after their little spat in the barn earlier.

"I have to go down," Peter said. "I can't wait until the morning."

"Knock if you need any help, all right? I'll be listening."

Peter made his way downstairs and found his second surprise of the night. Henry, looking stone cold sober, stood by the library doors with Jerry and Andrew to either side. When he saw Peter, he lowered his gaze to the floor. "I'd like you two gentlemen to leave me alone now," he said. His voice sounded raw, but solid. "I'd like to talk with Peter."

Jerry spoke in a soothing tone. "I don't know if that would be a good idea, Mr. Randolph. You've just had a hallucination. You're under a lot of stress. Sleep is the best course of action tonight."

"I'll sleep when I'm ready, Jerry. I am not a child, and I am not sick." The old man looked to Jerry with an unmovable expression. "I don't trust you. I think you're a scheming little coward who's lying to everybody in this house. This man, Andrew, included."

Jerry gave Andrew a look that said *they all get like this*.

Holy shit, Peter thought. *Is this guy for real?*

"We talked about your paranoia today, Henry, do you remember? In our one-to-one? Your little incident, the one about the boy, it's gotten you stressed out and worked up. You need to go to bed."

"Jerry. Leave me."

With a sigh, Jerry said, "All right, then, have it your way. But we'll talk more tomorrow. When you're feeling more like yourself. Andrew, come."

The two men left for the kitchen, taking the built up tension with them. When they were gone, Peter gave a curt nod. "You want to talk? The porch?"

"The porch sounds good."

The snow had decided to stay, after all, it seemed, and the grounds lay hidden beneath an untouched blanket that twinkled in the moonlight.

Henry shook his head. "We're stuck here. I had a feeling we'd be stuck here."

"You think it's that bad?"

"Look at it. I remember back in eighty-seven, a snow not nearly as bad hit. I tried to take my 4x4 down to the local store, needed some bread and such. Going slow, being very careful. Couldn't have been doing over twenty. Crashed into a neighbor's fence. The ice got me, packed beneath. We're at least an hour away from town. We're definitely stuck here."

Then he looked to Peter, his eyebrows drawing together. "I'm really sorry, Peter. I didn't mean to hit you."

"That's all right." Peter's chest hurt from the sincerity in the old man's face. He found it hard to understand, but he believed him. "I know you didn't."

"I wasn't drunk."

"Explain that."

"I can't. But I wasn't. I wouldn't dream of sneaking booze in here, you have to believe me. I *felt* drunk, but when I woke up downstairs, I felt fine. No hangover, no nothing. I call that a blessing. The most curious thing . . . I felt obliterated, but I hadn't had a single sip, I promise."

"So, what happened?"

Henry sighed. "Sit down with me. I have to tell you something."

Peter took the same bench he had the first night and Henry returned to the rocking chair. The icy wood made his buttocks clench so Peter slid his hands beneath him for heat. Cold hands seemed better than a cold ass.

Henry looked out to the still falling snow, his face unreadable. "I came here for one reason, and only one," he said, his breath coming away in a mist.

Peter nodded.

"Twenty years ago, I had a boy. But . . . I lost his mother in the process. I was inconsolable. She was a great lady, Peter. Lauren was her name. Lauren White." Henry's voice broke and he cleared his throat. "Soon to be Lauren White Randolph . . . My fiancée. Peter, you should have seen her. She had the thickest brunette hair you ever heard of, always tied up in a bun, and these eyes that were green as emeralds. Worked at the local pharmacy, loved her job, always had a keen interest in science. Chemistry and physics, mostly. I tell you, the amount of subscription magazines lying around the house would make you laugh. When she had to take maternity leave, she joked that I should be the one pregnant, seeing as how I didn't have a job and spent my time in the house anyway. An optimist to the end . . . And a wicked sense of humor, I might add. Not a day goes by that I don't miss her."

Peter let the memory run through Henry's mind. He saw it, too. Lauren White, the love of the old man's life, smiling and laughing without a care in the world, her eyes bright and all-too green. Henry sniffled, then he continued. "Doctors say it was eclampsia. She had seizures . . . High blood pressure . . . William was born prematurely, with Down syndrome."

Peter stayed silent, not knowing what to say.

"When things settled down . . . I'm sorry, if it's all right with you, I'd like to skip the Lauren part . . ."

"Of course."

Henry's eyes glistened as he wiped his nose with the back of his hand, his words catching in his throat. Peter decided to help him out. He knew exactly what to say.

"I'm going to be a father."

"You are?"

Peter smiled. "Yup . . . Beth . . . The only real friend I ever had. Known her since childhood. A while back, she got this new place, wanted me to come over and help her paint, you know? We rarely saw each other because I was off playing shows and stuff, but when she called, I was home. I went over. Things happened, and now this *big thing* is happening. A goddamn kid, can you believe it? I'm going to be a parent."

"You'd make a great father, Peter. And let me guess, this Beth girl, she's perfect, right?"

Peter chuckled. "No. She's not. She's clumsy, has a donkey's laugh, gets nervous too easy, and you know what? I think that's why I love her. She's real . . . I can be myself around her, just open up. I only hope I'm worth her time." He sniffled. "So, there's a reason for my being here."

Henry smiled. "Well thanks for sharing. I know it's hard to do."

"But, tit for tat, right?"

"Right." Henry's face fell. "It was just William and I, all the time. People will tell you they love their children no matter what, that they'd do anything for 'em, but I tell you, those people must be saints, because I didn't know this kid, and as far as I was concerned in my unstable state, he'd taken my Lauren and invaded my home. So, no, Peter, I didn't love him."

There was silence. Out in the night, unseen critters called and shuffled through the inky blackness as snow continued to fall.

"I wouldn't ever hurt him," Henry said, as if deflecting an unheard accusation. "Don't think I'm a monster. It's just, if I'm honest, I didn't love that baby. I didn't *feel* for him, not even if I tried. I couldn't force myself to . . . And so, I took to drinking. A lot. I could still function, get through the day mostly doing the normal-level things, but I was a zombie. Bills began piling up, and I couldn't stand to be with William. I know that makes me a bad person, but I just didn't love him and that's the truth. When he was six months old, he had a brain hemorrhage and died. Just a freak accident, but, Peter, I felt *relieved* . . . And happy, too, happy Lauren never had to see. She got spared that much. I was passed out on the couch at the time, about a half bottle of bourbon down, and I don't know if he cried, if he was awake, if he was scared, nothing. Lauren would be sick to her stomach if she knew what I became. And so, I need to change, for her. I need to set it right before it's too late and . . ." Henry took a deep breath. "What I saw tonight, Peter . . . I saw William."

A shiver crawled Peter's spine. "You *saw* him?"

"Clear as day. My baby boy. Right on my bed. I could even feel his weight on my chest. And I know how it *sounds*, it *sounds* insane, but I saw him. *I did*. And I felt drunk as hell, like I'd downed a whole bottle of bourbon in one. But I swear, I didn't even have a single sip of booze. I heard him laughing, giggling, and when I opened my eyes, my vision doubled, like a tank of alcohol just got dunked into my system. I started screaming and he laughed some more, and then the door opened. he disappeared. Just like that. Gone."

"I . . . I don't know what to say, Henry . . ."

"You think I'm crazy? You think I imagined it?"

"I don't know what to think."

Peter squirmed in his seat, the cold biting him. If what happened with Henry had been an isolated case he'd have an easier time understanding, but coupled with Walter the night before and with the Shelly Matthews missing, he had no clue. Peter decided to tell him about Shelly.

"And she was just gone?" Henry asked. "Nothing there?"

"Nothing there. And I know I didn't imagine that, because Donny, Walter, and Jamie all heard her, too. She screamed bloody murder. Sounded like she was ripping her vocal chords out. I thought she might need help, and Donny said to check on her. So I did. Just an empty room."

Henry looked back to the yard. He stayed quiet a long time. "Remember when we got here and I had a bad feeling? I said it to you because I saw something on your face that made me feel like I had to."

"I remember."

"It was more than just the fear of detox . . . Something about the farm scared me. Then that fog, it felt like a *presence*. It frightened me bad."

Peter decided to approach the idea of the fog with logic, wanting to cover all bases. "Don't laugh, but do you think we directed our fear at the fog, as a way of dealing with what we're feeling? Making something out of nothing to justify our worries?"

"No." Henry didn't pause a second. "Peter, there was something wrong with that fog. And now it's gone."

"Fogs go, Henry. Temperatures change, time moves on."

"Do I need to spell it out that much for you? Come on, Peter, wake up. It's gone, and on the same night, things started happening. Walter saw the ice cream man. I saw my boy. That girl is *missing*."

"Do you believe in the paranormal?" Peter asked.

"I believe in what I see. And from what I saw, that's the conclusion I've drawn. Do *you* believe in the paranormal?"

"No. But I agree something's happening here. A fog seems a little farfetched to me . . . But I do think Fisher's up to something. I just don't know what to do about it."

"First thing's first. We need to question him about Shelly Matthews, because she's here somewhere in this house. You heard her. If Jerry doesn't give us a straight answer, we call the police."

Peter agreed. Tomorrow, they'd question Jerry. They'd find out where Shelly Matthews had been taken. Because the idea of a third night in the Dawson farmhouse scared Peter half to death.

CHAPTER EIGHT

"I wee'd the bed because I dreamed of the ice cream man," Walter said. "That's why I did it."

Peter didn't think the man could any worse than the night before, but somehow he did. His skin seemed to droop from his bones, sagging and lifeless, while the whites of his eyes appeared yellow and streaked with veins. White patches streaked his dyed black.

He's scared half to death, Peter thought.

Jerry closed the morning's meeting with a clap of his hands. "You be brave now, Walter. Those dreams will pass." He smiled to the group. "Okay, was everybody happy with their job choice yesterday? Good to go to the same positions again today? Yes? No?"

The group grumbled an unenthusiastic yes.

"Good. Then have a good day, and I'll call you when lunch is prepared."

Like damn children, Peter thought, and left the room.

The group dispersed, Donald and Walter slogging towards the back door while Jamie went to the kitchen to help Paul with dishes. Peter spotted Jerry starting up the stairs. "Jerry," he called. "Henry and I would like a word with you, outside. Please."

Jerry flashed a smile that reminded Peter of a shark. "Certainly," he said, then led the way to the porch. Peter motioned to Henry, and the two men followed the counselor outside.

Earlier, at the meeting, Jerry had probed Henry about the previous night, but the old man had given as little detail as possible. He never mentioned the baby, or feeling blitzed. A breakdown, he'd told Fisher before the group, that's all. Then he apologized and said it wouldn't happen again. Judging by Jerry's strained smile, Peter knew the man hadn't believed Henry one bit.

At least five inches of snow covered the yard and Peter waded through it, wanting to be away from the house before confronting the counselor. He decided to skip pleasantries; he wanted to know Shelly Matthews' whereabouts, and he wanted to know now. Jerry arched an eyebrow. "What can I do for you, fellows?"

"Where is she?" Peter asked. "I heard her last night. Donny heard her. Walter and Jamie heard her. Even you heard her."

Jerry looked amused. "I assume you mean miss Matthews?"

Peter waited for Fisher to continue.

"Well, she was moved to our sister house in Pennsylvania during the night, if you must know. A wonderful place, specialized treatment, care, the works. We removed her from the house while you slept. Didn't want to upset the group. It's a lot to take on board, knowing that someone, someone the same as all of you, had to be removed from the house. Especially to those who are a little more sensitive than others. Poor mister Cartwright would keel over with such a stressful thought."

Henry stepped forward, narrowing his eyes to slits. "Look out at that road, Jerry. The road that isn't there. The place is smothered in snow. I know from experience, even in a 4x4, you might get down to town, sure, but there's no way you'd get back up. Not with how steep that hill is. Now, the bus was here all along, I saw it when I was out in the barn, and it hasn't moved. I would've heard that, I would've saw that. Nothing moved, and there are no tracks. Unless you flew a chopper up here, which we would all have been very aware of, then Shelly Matthews is still on this property."

Jerry let a moment pass before saying, "Shelly Matthews left for our sister clinic yesterday."

Peter's stomach roiled with disgust. "That's fine, Jerry. You want to play this game, we'll play."

Without another word to Fisher, Peter told Henry to follow and the two men made their way to the barn. Peter couldn't believe what just happened. Jerry had lied, and didn't seem bothered that two of the guests were onto him. Whatever that man had planned, Peter needed to know. He could feel the counselor watching them, his eyes slithering over their backs.

"Can you believe that?" Peter said. "He's not going to let up. We're going to have to get the police up here. I shouldn't have doubted you, Henry. I'm sorry."

"Don't worry about that now. Let's just get to the barn to clear our heads, give ourselves a minute. Then we go find a phone and get the hell out of here. Get our money back, too. And when Shelly Matthews shows up dead, let's sue this Dawson bastard for all he's worth. We can detox at my place when I have a pool built."

Peter chuckled. It felt good, even though it only took him out of the situation for a moment. "A nice big mansion," he said. "And a library filled with—" Peter paused. He had an idea.

"What's wrong?" Henry asked.

"The library. It's the only room we haven't been in yet, the one beside Fisher's office. Think she could be in there?"

"It's worth a shot. I mean, at the very least, the contents of those books . . ."

"The contents of those books, what? What is it?"

"You might think I'm crazy, but please, hear me out. What if there's something in that library other than psychology books, something about that fog and my hallucinations?"

"Walter's hallucinations, too," Peter said. "I don't know what we'll find there but it's worth a shot. Fisher's not going to play me for a fool."

"Damn right. Smug prick."

A scream rose from the house, making the hair on Peter's arms stand on end. Startled crows took flight from nearby trees.

Henry panted, a hand on his chest. "What was that?"

"Come on."

They made their way back to the farmhouse, their boots leaving a trail in the snow. Peter jogged at a slow pace to allow Henry to keep up, the old man's face turning red with the exertion. Donald came to the porch as they reached it, his skin pale, eyes wide.

"The kid, man," Donald spoke in a monotone. "James, Jamie, whatever his name is. Just bumped himself."

"Bumped himself?"

Peter and Henry climbed the porch.

"Glassed himself in the kitchen. Throat. Blood everywhere, man."

Fear dropped in Peter's stomach like an anchor. He felt lightheaded. "Where's Jerry?" he asked.

As if in answer, Jerry bounded through the hallway towards the kitchen. The three men watched the counselor in shock before following.

They took the dining area in quick stride, and as the kitchen door swung open, Peter skidded to a halt, taking two awkward steps back. Donald elbowed the door open again, entering the kitchen and giving Peter another glimpse of what lay beyond. A sight that hit him like a kick to the chest.

A hand clutched his shoulder. "Peter?" Henry said. "We don't have to go in there. You okay?"

"Y-yeah."

The floor had been painted red, shining in the overhead florescent light. Peter shook his head, trying to clear the image, but it was branded in the back of his eyelids. Jamie lay on his back, his neck in tatters. Ribbons of shredded skin were all that remained of his throat, reminding Peter of pulled pork. Glazed over eyes stared at the ceiling.

The room spun and Peter stumbled. He steadied himself and shut his eyes, feeling them vibrate beneath their lids. Henry put an arm around his shoulder.

"Come on, the hallway. Get out of the kitchen."

If Peter had said *okay*, he wasn't aware. Ringing blocked his ears and he fought to hold down what little breakfast he'd eaten. Now, in the hallway, he pressed his back to the wall.

"Why would he do that?" Peter's asked, his voice shaking. "He . . . He told me he had a girlfriend back home, a football team who needed him, he wanted to get back! He called us losers, that's the reason he punched me."

The dining-room door opened and Donald and Jerry joined them in the hallway, their faces flat and unreadable. Donald's skin looked the color of cottage cheese.

"What's happening here, Jerry?" Peter asked. His eyes stung with fresh tears. "*That kid wasn't suicidal.* I know that—you can't lie to me about it. Where's Shelly Matthews, and *what in the world is going on here?"*

"Peter, calm down."

"Calm down?" Peter pushed himself from the wall. "*Calm down*? You're holding something from us, man, something's going on here. And we want to know what it is!"

Peter was shocked to find himself holding Jerry by the scruff of the neck, pressing him into the wall. He hadn't planned on that, but he couldn't stop it. He mashed his forehead against Fisher's. "What the hell is going on around here! *Tell me!*"

"Kid, cut the shit!"

Donald grabbed him from behind and wrenched his arm back, sending a jolt of pain through Peter's bones. He doubled over as freeing Jerry panted, rubbing at his throat. It had turned red.

Donald freed Peter and barged into to the middle of the group, holding his hands out to separate them. "Now look, all right? Kid, you mess mister Fisher around, it ain't gonna do no good right now. I'm thinkin' practicality. We got a body that's gonna get stinky less we do somethin', you all understanding me? We need to phone a hospital and get an ambulance up here first. We'll deal with you later, Jerry. "

"The roads are off limits," Henry said. "We can't leave. We'll need them to bring in a helicopter."

"Well," Peter said. "Where's the phone, Jerry? When they get here, you're going to have to tell them about Shelly Matthews, too, because we are."

"In the library, Peter, and as I said, Shelly Matthews is gone to Pennsylvania to—"

"Oh fuck that noise."

Peter made for the porch. He slammed the door shut behind him and sucked cold air deep into his lungs. Adrenaline coursed through his body like a drug. He felt electric with rage, each breath making his chest shake. *He's a goddamn* liar, He thought. *Shelly's in this house somewhere . . .* The door opened, Henry and Donald joining him on the porch. They looked as annoyed and confused Peter he felt.

"Where's Fisher?" Peter asked.

"Back into the kitchen," Donald said. "With the black guy,

Paul. They're gonna sort out the mess. God knows where they're gonna put him. And kid, you got balls. Slammin' him against the wall and shit? What were you thinking?"

"I wasn't."

"I could see that." Donald ran a hand through his hair and sighed. "I didn't mean to hurt you, but if you touch Fisher you could mess up our plan. He'd have something to use against us if we were in the wrong. Not that I think we are, but just in case. Can't believe Jamie did that. I mean, I've seen it before, my older brother Harry? Hung himself over our second floor balcony when I was fifteen, but man, it was nowhere near as bad as that. Fuckin' gruesome. Christ."

Peter nodded. "I can't be here anymore. I can't take it. If Fisher comes back, tell him I'm in the library. I'm phoning the hospital and the cops."

Peter entered the house and heard Jerry and Paul's muffled voices come from the kitchen. He scanned the hall before making his way to the large double doors on the right, watching for any signs of Andrew Harper. The floorboards creaked beneath his feet. His heart punched his chest, its rhythmic thumping loud in his ears. Peter swallowed as he reached the doors and entered the room.

The familiar scent of pine air freshener greeted him, apparently the default smell of the house. Peter loathed it.

Rows of bookshelves occupied the room, five in total. A mismatch of ancient hardbacks and modern soft copies peppered the shelves with no rhyme or reason to their order. Some spilled on the floor, spread open like successful suicide jumpers.

Peter's spine crawled for no discernible reason. Despite the knocked-over books, the room looked like any other library he'd ever seen. *Except I'm not supposed to be in here*, He thought. *This is for Fisher only.*

Dim light came from a small window at the far side of the room and through it Peter saw an endless covering of white snow. *Snow that Fisher knew would stick . . . I need to find the phone.*

Peter made his way through the bookshelves, stepping

carefully over the spilled books. He glanced down every so often at their open faces.

Something struck him as odd.

The text wasn't English, in fact, most of it looked like a language Peter was unfamiliar with. Dirt and grime smudged the century old pages, cracks running their worn leather spines. Peter thought many looked in danger of falling to pieces at a single touch. As he continued on, he allowed his eyes to spill over their indecipherable messages.

He rounded the last bookshelf and spotted an old writing desk against a wall. More books were piled high on its surface, and in the center sat an open journal. A gooseneck lamp loomed over the journal, and Peter reached to switch it on when something else caught his eye.

A dial-up telephone. He smiled.

Peter knew that even if the snow cut the electricity, a dial-up would work regardless, due to the phone lines. He decided to start with the police, but didn't know what to say.

Hi, I'm a strung-out alcoholic currently undergoing rehabilitation, and I don't trust my counselor.

No good.

My friend saw his dead baby crawling over him last night . . . Another guy, fresh off antidepressants, saw an ice cream man from his childhood who might've been a child molester!

For god's sake . . . Peter decided to wing the conversation. He placed his hand on the receiver, and then the phone rang.

Peter picked it up straight away, an automatic reaction to its shrill cry. His heart beat his chest as the ringing echoed though the room.

"Hello?"

"Peter?"

A cocktail of relief and confusion rushed through his body at the sound of the woman's voice. Peter licked his lips. They felt too dry. "Grandma?"

"Peter, it's me. How are you? Are you settled in yet?"

Peter couldn't find his voice, the situation overwhelming. Should he tell her about Jerry Fisher? About Walter and his night terror? Or Henry? Or even worse, Jamie Peters' suicide? Thoughts wheeled around inside his head like loose laundry inside a washing machine. Then Peter found his voice. "How did you get this number?"

He listened to his grandmother breathing, a harsh labored sound, followed by a clicking of the throat. Then, slowly, she began to laugh.

"Oh Peter, it's a good thing your poor mother died so she didn't have to see what a fuck-up you became."

Peter's stomach dropped. His legs attempted to buckle beneath him but he managed to stand.

"You're a loser, Peter," she said. "We both know this little trip of yours wouldn't work out. Just something for you to try and feel like you're resolving your problems when really it's nothing more than a temporary feel-better. A rolling stone gathers no moss, remember that one? And Peter, you're so covered in moss that I'm surprised you can move at all. It's growing from your pores like the hair on your arms. It's everywhere, we can all see it. Don't think you're hiding. We're all laughing at you, the only thing we can't agree on is when your body is finally going to be found!"

A scream ripped Peter's throat. His knuckles turned white as his grip tightened on the receiver. "Why would you say this to me? *Why?*"

"Because you need the truth and the truth hurts, little boy." The old woman laughed again, and Peter wanted to vomit. He'd heard that laugh a thousand times before, but this time it was an alien thing, full of sinister sickness. She was laughing *at him*.

Peter's chest heaved, his stomach struggling to hold its contents. He tried for words but found none.

The old woman continued. "Why don't you just do us both a favor and kill yourself? End it. End it, Peter. Do it for me. Do it for Beth, and do it for the lovely little baby, so it will never have to be ashamed it had such a *fuck-up* for a father. You were right the first time, and you were so close, too. We were nearly done with you. Your burden . . . Until you saw this stupid rehabilitation advertisement. Fuck, I was nearly rid of you once and for all . . ."

Peter's head rocked from side to side. He still had nothing to say.

"That Jamie Peters had guts. He did it. Why can't you? Beth would be *so* happy. She could find a *real* man and forget all about you. Then again, she'll probably do that anyway. She's far, far too good for you."

Something clicked in Peter's head. His eyes grew wide. "How would you know about Jamie Peters?" he asked. "Huh? How would you know?"

The old woman's laughter became a cackle and Peter moved the earpiece away from his head, the shrill sound making him cringe.

"Who are you?"

"*Ooowwww,*" The old woman mocked. "I'm your Gwandma, siwy? Poor frail old Gwandma . . . Lost her daughter and gained a fuck-up." She sighed. "And what a fuck-up you are, too, I mean, holy crap!"

Peter roared over the woman's cackle, "Shut up! You're not my grandmother!"

He almost shoved the mouthpiece of the phone inside of his mouth. "Stop it!"

"Peter!"

Henry's voice came from the doorway and Peter wheeled around. The old man stood with Donald Bove, both of them looking terrified. Peter hadn't heard the door open. Sweat dripped from his forehead and his chest heaved.

This what it feels like to pass out? he wondered.

"It's the phone," he said, his voice sounding like sandpaper. "My grandmother."

Then the world turned black.

CHAPTER NINE

"Peter? Peter? I think he's waking up. Donald, bring it here."

Peter's mind swam back to consciousness. A wet cloth pressed against his forehead, the cold water running down his face. He opened his eyes.

"He's awake, Don. We're good."

"Where am I?"

Peter's voice still sounded like his vocal chords had been replaced by a bag of grit. It stung to speak. "Water, please."

Henry nodded. Sitting up, Peter saw that he lay on the couch in the living room. He didn't know what he'd expected, definitely not a hospital, not with the snow outside, but a part of him still felt nauseous at the sight of the room. He hoped things maybe had corrected themselves while he'd been out, but no. He was still in the farmhouse.

"Sit up," Henry said as he returned with the water. "Drink this."

Peter accepted the glass and took two large gulps. The cold water coated his raw throat, burning and soothing. He decided to sip the rest.

"What . . . What happened?"

"You blacked out, kid." Donald sat with his hands together on the other couch, watching Peter with narrow eyes. "Just went up and over when we found you into the library. Heard you shoutin' from the porch. Just looked at us, mumbled somethin', and *boom*. Down for the count."

"Really?" Peter rubbed at his eyes. "And Jerry? Where's Jerry?"

Henry and Donald exchanged a glance that made Peter's heart race. "What? What is it?"

"That's just it," Henry said. "We don't know."

"What do you mean?"

Henry's lips tightened. "When we brought you in here, we

heard something from the kitchen, banging and such. But when we went in there . . . He was gone. Tracks were smeared in the kid's blood, like his body'd been dragged around, but he was gone, too. All three of them. No sign of Jerry Fisher, no sign of that man, Paul, and no sign of the dead kid. All three are just . . . Gone."

A nightmare, Peter decided. *I've woken up into a damn nightmare.*

Part of him wanted to close his eyes and slip back into sleep. He wanted out of this place, wanted to be safe at his grandmother's house. He wanted Beth. "How can that be?" he asked. "Any track marks outside?"

"We checked out back," Donald said. "No trace in the snow. Kid, even if it's falling heavy, there's just no way their prints would be covered that quick. You know what I'm gettin' at? They're still in this house. My money's on where that Matthews gal is at."

Peter's forehead creased as he digested the information. No sign of Jerry or his assistant, with Jamie Peter's body missing, too. If Fisher'd taken the kid outside, the blood marks on the snow would be clear. Donald and Henry would have noticed. That left only one option . . .

"They're still in the house," Peter said. "We just need to figure out where." He looked to Henry. "What time is it?"

"Quarter past nine. You've been out the whole day."

Peter's stomach tightened. "Past nine? Really? Where's Walter?"

"Asleep in his room," Donald answered. "He's in a bad way, man. Real bad. Didn't bat an eyelid at the all the blood in the kitchen. Trust me, when I told him what'd happened, he just nodded and made for his room. Ain't right, man. Been up there for at least three hours now. Mumbled something about not feelin' good. We were gonna check on him before you woke up. Wanna join us?"

"Okay," Peter agreed. "But are we the only ones left? The three of us, and Walter?"

"That man, Andrew? He's still here." Henry said. "And he's a good man from what I can tell. Call that intuition again. Didn't know anything about Jerry Fisher or the Dawson clinic before coming here, that's for sure. Seemed just as scared as the rest of us when he saw the blood. Started saying he had a wife and little girl back home and just wanted to get back to 'em. Managed to calm him down, eventually. He shook something fierce."

Donald nodded in agreement. "Either he's honest to god just as freaked out as the rest of us, or he's an academy-award-winning actor. But I'm going out on a limb here and say he's fuckin' scared. He's on the porch now, drinking a cup of coffee, keepin' watch. Night-owl by nature. Part of why he took the job, he says. Said he'd keep watch for any signs of anything out there."

"What's he looking out for exactly?"

Henry crossed his arms. "You know, Peter."

That damned fog . . .

"Plus," Henry added. "Sometimes a man just needs to be with his thoughts. Let him process this, because I trust him. He'll be ready when he's ready. For now, we need to check on Walter."

"Sure."

Henry leaned forward. "Pete, you want to tell us what happened in the library?"

"It was my grandmother."

Donald arched an eyebrow. "What's that?"

"On the phone, I mean. She called when I tried to phone the cops, but it wasn't *her*. It *sounded* like her, but it wasn't her, I was—"

"Easy, easy," Henry said, placing a hand on Peter's shoulder. "After Walter's episode, and mine, you don't need to explain yourself to us."

"I'm sorry I doubted you, Henry."

"Don't worry about it. We tried the phone, it's not even working."

"You think Fisher cut the lines?"

"Most definitely. He took our cell phones, after all." Henry stood. "Come on, let's just check on Walter."

The three of them made their way upstairs, Peter stopping twice due to dizzy spells. The grandfather clocked chimed from downstairs and the smell of pine still held thick in the air, making his head throb. The humming pain in his cheek and nose from the punches he'd received earlier didn't help matters, either. And now the back of his head joined in. The blow must have been rough to keep him out cold for nearly the whole day. He worried about a concussion but pushed the thought aside for the task at hand. They reached Walter's room and entered with a fragile knock of the door.

"Come in . . ." Walter slurred, his voice weighed down by sickness.

"Walter," Peter said with a smile. "How're you feeling?" He tried to refrain from sounding shocked, but what he saw turned his stomach.

Walter sat propped against his headboard, the pillows cushioning his large back. His dyed black hair, now streaked with white, looked glued into place by sweat. His glasses sat askew on his nose, his eyes sunken into his skull, ageing him by at least a decade. Red patches blotched his face, as if he'd recently scratched it. As his enormous chest rose and fell, he wheezed like a clogged engine.

"The ice cream man was back," he said. "Came into the stables while I made up a bed for Alisa . . . A real nice one, too, but he frightened me so bad and . . . When I saw him, it felt like someone was running jagged fingers up my spine, can you picture that? My hairs were standing up, all on the back of my neck . . . But I stayed calm and came back to the house, thinking *he's not there, he's not there* . . . But then he followed, staying right behind me with that horrible jaw swinging, and then he *laughed!* Can you believe that? I jumped a mile into the air, and then he asked if I'd like a treat . . ."

Walter sighed. "I told him no, I was too old for treats, because I'm an adult now. But he just kept laughing and laughing . . . So I came inside and decided to go to bed. He can't get me when I sleep. He's not in my dreams. I'm alone there. But he's still here, in the house. But, you know what? I didn't pee myself this time, isn't that something? You can feel for yourself, my sheets are dry, honest."

"That's okay, Walter," Peter said. His heart went out to the man. Walter reminded him of a scared child trapped inside an adult body, a real-life Peter Pan who didn't seem to understand how the world worked. Or maybe he *did* understand but didn't care, because he couldn't change. Either way, it all amounted to the same thing: Here lay a frightened person in need of comfort, and if that didn't happen, he might be scared to death.

"What do you mean he's still here?" Donald asked.

"I mean," Walter said, "that he's still in the house. You guys scared him when he heard you coming. Scuttled out of the room like a rat because he didn't want to get caught. That's what I think . . . You didn't see him?"

"No," Peter said, shaking his head. "I don't think there's anyone in the house that we don't know about, Walter, don't worry."

"Okay, then . . ."

Walter closed his eyes and took a deep breath that rattled inside his chest. He pulled his covers up high, making him appear like a floating head. "Then I guess I can sleep."

A crash came from the hallway. Peter's body stiffened. "What was that?"

The four of them listened, their eyes wide. The grandfather clock ticked downstairs, heavy breathing filled the room, but nothing else. The silence suspended.

Henry licked at his lips before he spoke, keeping his voice down. "We should check that out . . . Sounded like it was on the second floor. One of us should stay with Walter."

Peter turned to Donald and nodded towards the door, arching his eyebrows in a question: *You coming with me?*

Donald nodded before following. Creeping to the door, Peter eased it open and cringed as the hinges squeaked. He tiptoed into the hallway and looked both ways. Shelly Matthews' door stood ajar.

"There," he whispered.

Making his way to the door, Peter breathed through his mouth to control his airflow, wanting to make as little noise as possible. His heartbeat drummed in his ears, loud enough for the whole house to hear. Then something moved inside of Shelly's room. A black figure shifting in the dark. Peter squinted and quickened his pace. Behind him, Donald did the same, until the two men were sprinting for the door, no longer worried about being heard.

Peter smashed the door with his knee, sending it crashing to the wall. He fumbled with the light switch, knocking it down and shocking the room with light. Then he saw it. Only for a second, but he saw it. Donald must have, too, because a string of curse words spewed from his mouth. Peter's mind reeled. It couldn't have been real . . . *Couldn't have.*

A dark fog, inky and terrible, shot through the laundry shoot near the window, disappearing as if a vacuum had been switched on. But something in Peter's mind told him otherwise—the fog hadn't been sucked through. It had slithered all by itself. It had run.

"Did you fuckin' see that?"

Peter placed a hand on his chest, trying to ease his heart. "Yeah. I did."

"What the fuck was that thing? It was *alive!*"

Henry shouted from the hallway. "What's going on?"

"We saw something!" Peter answered. Donald tapped his shoulder. "Come on, man. I've got the fuckin' creeps."

They made their way back to Henry, Peter's legs moving like water damaged planks. His nerves sung, his hair prickling and standing on end; having his back to the room made him feel all too exposed.

Henry watching them with an anxious look. "What was it? What happened?"

Peter couldn't believing the words coming from his own mouth, his brain wouldn't allow it. "The fog," he said. "Henry, you were right. It went through the laundry shoot."

"I told you," Henry said. "I knew it. Donald, I told Peter all about it. That damned fog wasn't natural, I could *feel* it. You know that feeling when you think somebody's watching you? That's what it felt like when I saw it from the porch . . . But I chalked it up to paranoia from lack of nicotine and alcohol. I should have trusted my gut. You believe in the paranormal, Donny?"

"After what I just saw, man, space aliens, werewolves, whatever, I'll listen. That thing's out to get us."

Henry turned to Peter. "Peter? What did you make of it?"

Peter stayed silent as he toyed with a concept in his mind. He decided to tell them. "I think Walter *did* see the ice cream man . . . But I think that none of *us* would see an ice cream man . . . I think you *did* see your son, Henry, but I think Donald and I wouldn't see your son . . . I think we're seeing what we don't want to see . . . What we fear . . . Look, I know it sounds crazy, and maybe it is, but—"

"Fisher," Henry said, his eyes bright. "That sonofabitch . . ."

"What? What is it?"

"Our counselling sessions . . . He was milking us for information, finding out what frightens us the most. Think about it, Walter told him all about the ice cream man *before* he got attacked. I told him all about my son, just before—"

Peter interrupted. "You *told* him about that?"

"Yes . . . After our argument, I thought, maybe I am just paranoid. I gave in. I told him all about why I'm here when we had our one-to-one. And you, did you tell him about your grandmother?"

"He already knew. Dawson did a background check on all of us."

"What's the bet Jamie was terrified of fucking it all up, huh?" Donald ask. "What's the bet that dark shit got inside his head, made him think bad thoughts?"

"If we're going with our theory, then I think it's highly likely . . ." Peter looked to them both. "Jamie wanted to get out of here as soon as possible. Deep down, he must have been afraid of losing himself to the meds. That *thing* must have known that. Got inside his mind, *infected* him, turned him against himself, made him see no way out . . . Either that or I'm just tweaking the fuck out . . ."

"I don't think so," Henry said. "I don't want to believe it, but it's adding up."

Peter blew a deep breath. "Come downstairs, there's something I want to check out."

"What is it?"

"A notebook on the table in the library. There's writing in it, books scattered all over the place. We could find some answers."

"Hey," Donald said. "What about Walt? Can't leave the poor fuck up here."

Peter rubbed his forehead. "You're right . . . Let's get him out of bed, put him downstairs. We can keep an eye on him in the living room."

"Good idea."

They went back inside Walter's room, turning on the light as they entered. They froze.

Walter's condition had deteriorated at a staggering pace. Beneath the bedsheets moved what looked like a decomposing corpse, Walter's skin glazed in sweat and the color of spoiled milk. His eyes darted around the room, unable to stay put.

He's panicking, Peter thought.

"Walter!" Peter ran to the bedside. "Walter, speak to me. You hear me?"

The large man's chest rattled as it rose, his breath smelling sweet and sick. He grabbed Peter's arm.

"What's happening? Feels like my brain is getting sick inside my head! I don't feel right!"

"It's all right, Walter, we're going to get you downstairs and get you better, okay? Hold onto me." He turned his head. "Guys, help."

Henry and Donald raced to his side, Donald throwing Walter's bedsheets to the floor in a heap. Walter's white pajama pants stuck to his legs with moisture, his hairy stomach dripping and shining. He was right about one thing, though—he hadn't wet the bed.

"Come on, big guy," Donald said, then the three pulled Walter to his feet. He staggered, almost falling forward if Donald hadn't been quick enough. He caught Walter around the waist and wrenched him back, throwing an arm around his neck and looking to Peter to do the same. He did. They held the sick man between them as Henry jogged to the door and held it open.

Walter weighed a ton. His legs dragged the floor, twitching as they sought purchase. He moaned, his head rocking about on the stalk of his neck. Heat radiated from his glistening flesh and Peter turned his head away, avoiding the warmth.

"There we go," Peter said, feeling the need to talk. "You stay focused now, Walter. Move your feet to help us out, okay? We're going to get you downstairs."

Walter moaned, then vomited. The liquid splashed the hardwood before jumping onto Peter's jeans and boots. The smell was enough to make Peter hold his breath. Donald seemed to struggle, too.

Peter groaned. "Come on . . . Into the hallway . . . That's it, keep moving."

They angled themselves for the staircase, lurching in an awkward shuffle. Then Walter fell slack, the deadweight on Peter's shoulder unbearable. His knees shook and he grunted, looking to Donald.

"Down, down, down," Donald spat, lowering Walter as he spoke. The sick man's legs folded like an accordion on the ground. A horrifying thought struck Peter so quick that his own legs nearly did the same.

"Is he?"

"Yeah, he is. Now put 'em down."

Peter stepped away and pressed his back to the wall, wiping the sweat from his brow. "He's dead?"

He knew the answer, of course, but the question still fell from his mouth.

"Dead as a stump."

Donald rolled his sleeves and looked to the other two. He cocked an eyebrow. "Rigor mortis gonna set in pretty fast. We can do one of two things here, and I need you both to stay calm and not freak until we get this done, all right? You can lose your shit pretty easy in this kind of situation, but if you stay focused, we can get the job finished. We'll freak afterwards, okay? There'll be time for that. Just don't do it now."

Peter and Henry both nodded, silent.

"All right then. First choice." Donald raised a finger. "We put him back in his room, hope someone shows up and saves the day. But I don't think that's fuckin' likely. That's option number one. Second choice," He raised another finger. "We move him outside, because I don't think I need to tell you twice, if he's up here and we're stuck in this house on account of the snow, he's gonna stink up the joint. And that's a smell you never forget, swear on my mother's good name. Ain't gonna wanna smell that shit for all the money in the world."

"We get him out," Henry said, his voice shaking. "Peter?"

"Outside. Right."

Donald nodded. "Good choice. In that case, kid, grab the poor fuck's legs. I'll get the top half. Henry? Make sure the path's clear and there ain't nothin' we can fall over, all right?"

"Sure." Henry went down the staircase ahead of them.

"All right, let's do this."

They hoisted the dead man, Donald's muscles bulging.

Jesus, Peter thought. *How much can Walt weigh?*

Donald's face strained, turning red. "Heavy sumbitch, ain't he?" He wrinkled his nose in disgust. "Bet you didn't know your bowels evacuate when you kicked the bucket, eh?"

Walter may not have wet the bed, but he had destroyed his pajama pants with something much worse. Peter felt awful, but he'd have time to deal with his emotions later. Right now, he needed to get the body down the stairs.

They took the steps at a calculated pace, Peter concentrating on the handrail as a point of focus to distract him from the immense weight in his arms. Walter's stomach jiggled with each movement, his mouth hanging open.

Catching Peter's expression, Donald sighed. "There's no fuckin' dignity in this, I know, kid. Just keep movin'."

As they made their way into the open cold, their breath streamed away in visible clouds. Darkness surrounded them as the snow crunched beneath their feet. Peter's hands were numb.

"Where to?" Peter asked. He needed to drop Walter soon or his arms would give out.

"Can't go too far, might attract animals. I know he's dead, but it's the least we can do for the poor fuck. We'll bury him in some snow for now . . . Put him on ice, y'know?"

Peter ignored the comment.

"Kid, it's a joke. Look, we'll dig a proper grave when there's some light. Good?"

Peter nodded. "Yeah. All good."

They were a few feet from the house when Peter's stomach fluttered. He looked to Donald. "Where's Andrew?"

CHAPTER TEN

"Use the bus as a marker," Peter said, his heart racing. "Count ten paces and cover him. We need to find Andrew."

Donald nodded and counted his steps. "Here. This'll do."

They worked fast, shoveling snow with their bare hands until Walter disappeared beneath the white mound. With the job done, Peter's hands shook, his skin red and numb.

"Come on," Henry said, leading the way to the farmhouse. He called out. "Andrew!"

They climbed the porch and entered the hallway, scanning the building. "Let's check the kitchen," Peter said, shaking his hands. They tingled and stung. "We should start downstairs."

A mumble drifted from the library. A man's voice, low and wavering.

"Sounds like crying?" Donald said. "Come on."

The hallway light cut a sliver through the dark room, illuminating open books on the hardwood. Andrew stood in the dull light, the phone pressed to his ear. "—But you can't," he said. The bearded man looked to them, his cheeks shining with tears. "She can't, right?"

Peter kept his voice steady. "Andrew, drop the phone. Whoever you think you're talking to, you're not. I promise."

"No, it's her. It's my wife. She's taking my son away. She's met somebody. Somebody better than me."

"Andrew, drop the phone," Peter insisted. "Do it."

Looking like a zombie, the large man lowered the receiver back to the cradle, shaking his head. "Said she met him at her art class. Had more in common . . . Said he had more time for her." Andrew wiped his nose on his shirtsleeve. "She said he knew about art and that all I cared about was football and such . . . Didn't even say what such was. Thinks I don't pay enough attention to her." His lip quivered. "But I love her art, I do, I just don't know any names or anything . . ." Andrew cradled his face in one large palm.

Peter stepped forward. "It wasn't her, Andrew. I promise. There's something inside the house, feeding off our fears. Look, it's getting into our heads, that's all. Ruining us from the inside out. I promise you, that was not your wife . . ." Peter licked at his lips. "That man, Walter, just died."

Andrew removed his hand from his face, his eyes swollen. "What?"

"He's dead. We buried him outside."

"What's happened?"

"We don't know, but we're trying to figure it out. Will you help us?"

"What are you talking about? What use am I?"

"Four heads better than three," Donald said. "We're as lost as you are, man, but we've got some clues. Help us."

Peter nodded. "I got a phone call, too, from my grandmother. But it wasn't her, Andrew. Just like that wasn't your wife."

"I've imagined her saying those things to me so many times" Andrew said. "I've tried to learn the names of artists but they wouldn't stay in my head . . . I've just been waiting for this day. She seemed so happy every time she came home from her classes. I know I could never make her smile like that and it hurt to know she was getting her happiness elsewhere. I just wanted to try and make her smile like that class did. But I never could. Not the way she smiled coming home. I know I work too much, but I don't know what else to do, there's so many bills to pay, and with Ivan only six months old . . ."

"It's all right," Peter said. "We'll figure this out."

"Hey . . ." Donald squinted down at one of the open books. "Think Fisher threw them all over like this? Lookin' for somethin'? You know, like, flung them around when he couldn't find what he needed?"

Peter plucked one from the floor at random and skimmed the pages. His skin broke out in gooseflesh at the touch, each page feeling dusty and thick.

Like it's made of skin, Peter mused. *This is disgusting . . .*

"What's it say?" Henry asked.

"I don't know. Looks like Latin to me . . . But I never made it past basic French in school. No chance of understanding it."

He turned another yellowed page, revealing an illustration. "What's this?"

Peter angled the book beneath the sliver of hall light to show the others.

"Looks like a frog-man," Donald said. "Some sort of daemon or some shit."

Peter leaned closer to the page to study the sketch. The creature hunched, knees bent, as if its legs struggled to carry the weight of its bulging upper half. Its slim arms reached to its kneecaps, the webbed fingers capped with ragged nails. Beady, fish-like eyes sat to either side of its bulbous head, and a fin ran from the tip of its crown down its back. Its mouth hung open to reveal rows of jagged teeth.

"It reminds me of The Deep Ones," Peter said. "From a H.P. Lovecraft story. The ones from Innsmouth."

Donald arched an eyebrow. "The who from the what?"

"The Deep Ones. Amphibious creatures that used to be people. It's a strange story. When I was on tour, I heard that a lot of bands used H.P. Lovecraft as an influence for their lyrics. We had plans for a second album and I was dry when it came to lyrics so I read all of his stuff. The writing's a little dated but the stories are good. This thing looks like one of his creatures, one of The Deep Ones."

"Are you *holding* a H.P. Lovecraft book?" Henry asked.

Peter flipped the cover, the brown leather cracking. He scanned the small gold print, trying to decipher the faded title. "Nah . . . Looks to be in Latin, too. But I don't think it's Lovecraft. Lovecraft's covers would be modern reprints, not some worn out old dusty thing like this. I mean, it looks like a bible or something . . . No way he'd have been translated to Latin back when this thing was published. It's old, Henry."

"So what do you reckon?" Donald asked. For the first time, Peter thought the man sounded frightened.

"I have no idea," he said. "But I think we should gather up a few and take them to the living room. There's a notebook on the table by the phone, do you see it, Andrew? Good. Grab that, too."

Donald swiped a handful of the books from a shelf. "Now

let's leave. Gettin' the willies here, kid."

They managed fifteen titles between them before making their way to the living room. Once there, they dumped them to the rug and spread out on the couches. The fire had died, leaving a sharp chill in the air.

"Any logs?" Henry asked. "There were logs stacked here yesterday."

"That was my job," Andrew confessed. "I didn't get around to doing it today. Not with what's been happening, I'm sorry."

"Don't worry about it," Peter said. "We can grab some blankets from upstairs if it starts getting cold. Right now, I just want to see what all this is all about."

He started with the notebook, the kind of ledger found in any gas station for a dollar. Besides being new, the book gave the same feeling as the other.

Dirty and wrong . . .

Peter scanned the first page:

The five subjects are good. They're grasping for straws. It's pretty pathetic, actually.

"Oh my God . . ." Peter tore his eyes from the page. "It's all here. Fisher's own words."

"What's it say?" Donald asked.

"Listen to this, he's keeping track of everything."

Donald rolled his finger. "Well fuckin' read it out!"

"It says . . . *There's one man, Walter Cartwright, about forty-six or so, fat with big glasses. He's a mess. I'm sure he'll be the first to go. Phobos will settle nicely in this one. If he can control himself this time.*" Peter lowered the book. "*Phobos?*"

The three men shook their heads. He continued.

"*I prepared the first host simply as a tester. But my concerns turned out to be true. Phobos couldn't control Himself. Too eager . . . The heroin addict, Shelly Matthews, succumbed to terrible withdrawal on the first night. I took her to the basement and did it. I followed Dawson's instructions to the letter.*" Peter looked to Andrew. "The basement? Where's the basement, Andrew?"

The large man's forehead creased. "I swear, I didn't even know this place *had* a basement. Honest."

Peter turned his attention back to Jerry's notebook. "*It was messy,*" he read. "*She didn't know what was happening. The other guests were in bed, so getting her down took some effort. When she awoke, she kicked the place apart. Nearly broke one of my tables, destroyed my things. I had to be quick. I sliced her throat. Collected the blood in a copper basin, just as instructed, and then . . . Then I saw magic . . . I was wrong to ever doubt Dawson. When I checked again, the blood had disappeared. Phobos is here! He's alive!!!*"

"Sweet Jesus," Henry said, raising a shaking hand to his mouth. "He killed that poor woman . . ."

When Peter looked back to the page, he noticed his own hands trembling. He continued reading. "*I can handle this just fine. It won't take me too long, which is good, because I think I might have underestimated a couple of the candidates. Henry Randolph, the old guy, he's wising up to something, and he's got the younger one (a pathetic loser in his thirties) convinced. They're conspiring. I'm chalking it up to them being paranoid, trying to cement that in their minds at our one-to-ones. Thought that excuse would work, but they're seeing through. I need to be quick.*"

"I knew it from day one," Henry said, his voice flat. "The heartless, *pathetic* bastard. How dare he."

"Let me get to the end, Henry." Peter licked his lips and cleared his throat. "*I'll keep working at that, but right now Jamie Peters has my attention. He spilled everything to me at our counseling session, everything. I got it all. He's seventeen with a hard-ass for a father and a mother who pays no attention, blah blah. The usual story we've all heard a thousand times. The kid rebelled by hosted pharming parties but ended up getting caught . . . Wound up here, telling me all about it. Telling Phobos all about it.*

"*And it's happened; already, today, I saw Phobos working on him. I don't think Jamie can fight it. I wonder what my Lord showed him? I wish we could see that part. The kid's weak, and once he goes down, I'll prepare his body as our second host, because, as I said, Shelly did not work out. Christ, what a mess . . . The corpse was too small, too frail, but still, Phobos tried. An amazing sight!"*

"What did he do?" Donald asked.

"Her body lay on the table, lifeless. Then, out of nowhere, it jittered as if someone put a pump inside, inflating her, filling up . . ."

Peter took a deep, unsteady breath. *"Her head began changing shape, like putty moving all by itself . . . She screamed, or at least, Phobos screamed using her mouth. I didn't expect that to happen with Phobos being so weak. The act must have been agonizing. After a while, it just stopped. All of it. My Lord tried, but Shelly wasn't a match. Her body's a used-up mess now. The bones are broken, the skin stretched . . . doesn't even look human. I'll discard of the corpse soon enough . . .*

I can't get used to writing manually but at Harris' request I'm doing it. I'm still reading up in the library. Half pulled it apart for more information."

Peter lowered the book and looked to the others. Henry's eyes glistened and shook. Donald stared at the wall, his face unreadable. Andrew looked frightened and confused, like a man experiencing a bad dream.

"What do you make of that?" Peter asked.

Andrew smacked his hand down on the couch. "It's the ramblings of a mad man!"

"Hey!" Henry said. "If I hadn't seen what I've seen with my own two eyes, I'd agree with you. One hundred percent. But that's not the case and you know it because of that phone—"

"I haven't seen anything!" Andrew interrupted. "Nothing! All I know is that my wife called. She's leaving me! That's what I know, and as hard as that is to believe, it's a hell of a lot easier a pill to swallow than believing in a god named *Phobos* who hosts inside human bodies!"

Donald chuckled. "It sounds insane, man, I won't correct you there, but . . ." He turned to Andrew then, his expression serious. "Shut the fuck up and let the man finish reading, now. You hearin' me?"

Andrew nodded without a word.

"Good," Donald said. "Pete, continue, please."

Peter did. *"I hope Phobos knows how hard I'm working for*

Him. I hope He can see that. I hope he reward me because I do deserve it. Very soon, He can try to host again. This time in the boy's body. The only thing I'm worried of is the boy's age. He's so young . . . His bones might be too fragile to take the transfer, even though he's built like a brick shithouse. We'll see . . . If not him, then another. Either way, I think we can do this. That Walter one is losing his mind already, hallucinating. He said something about an ice cream man on the first night, that's when I knew Phobos was in the house. He showed Walter a molesting childhood ice cream man! Ha! I could hardly contain my excitement. And . . . I saw Him, in His raw state, but my brain could only perceive Him as a black fog . . . Reading all these tales is one thing, but seeing it for real? My god, it's magnificent."

Peter lowered the notebook and thumbed the rest of the pages. "All blank," he said. "This is Fisher's first one."

"We're like goddamn mice for a snake here," Donald said. "That's exactly it, ain't it? Mice for a motherfuckin' pet snake. Jumpin' talkin' Jesus." He shook his head. "Where is this fuckin' Phobos? Eh? I've had enough of this shit. I ain't waitin' around to be a snack or a . . . a fuckin' shell! Let's find the bastard."

"Donny." Peter kept his voice calm. "We need to stay level headed. Keep our wits about us. Let's gather together what we know."

"It was all a ruse," Henry said. "Dawson and Fisher, they're some sort of religious servants to this god, this *Phobos*. A creature that feeds on fear . . . That's why Fisher counseled us one by one. He separated us out, getting us to open up to him. Me seeing my son, Walter seeing the ice cream man . . . It all makes sense now. We were giving ammo to that creature. He's getting inside our heads to scare us to death."

"He needs a host body," Peter added. "Like he needs to find a good *fit*. Shelly's body wasn't good enough for him. And Jamie? who knows. His neck is sliced, but he *is* young . . ."

Donald leaned forward. "Yo. You all right, kid?"

"Yeah." Peter smiled sheepishly. "I know this isn't the time for it, but I think my brain is screaming for a cigarette . . . Can feel the oxygen in my system, making me feel a little lightheaded. I'll be fine."

"I've been the same, don't worry about it. Keep thinking of something else."

"I thought you guys would be a bunch of tweakers," Andrew said. "Honest. I thought you'd be, I don't know, different."

"Don't judge someone on one bad life choice," Henry said. "Can go stale for anyone and at any time. Might be down, but we're not out."

"Damn right," Donald said. He stood. "And we're going to find this sumbitch and whoop his ass. Ancient fuckin' god or not, if its standin' and breathin' I'll knock its fuckin' teeth loose. Where we gonna find the bitch, eh?"

"I don't think we need to find him," Henry said. His face dropped, his face shining with sweat. He pointed to the window. "I think he's just found us."

"You're shittin' me . . ."

Outside, Walter tapped the glass, and smiled.

CHAPTER ELEVEN

The snow settled on Walter's bare shoulders, his skin anemic and goose-pimpled. His glasses fogged with the cold, and his once-dyed black hair, now mostly white, stood up in awkward clumps. He smiled, pressing his face to the window. "It sure is cold out here, guys. Aren't you going to let me in?"

Peter's spine crawled, like cold ants scuttling beneath his clothes. He stood shoulder to shoulder with the others, watching the grinning corpse. The logical side of his brain tried to tell him that this was all a very real dream, brought about by the stress of going cold turkey. It had to be. But he knew his own mind well, and this was real as real could be. Outside, a dead man walked.

"You said he'd *died*," Andrew shouted, pointing towards the window. "You idiots! What have you done?"

"Andrew!" Henry's face turned red, his nostrils flaring. "It's a trick. That's *all* it is. That *thing*, that *Phobos* has hosted inside of him, haven't you been listening to a thing Peter said?"

The corner of Andrew's lips curled in a smirk. "I've been listening, all right, but all I see is a cold man, old-timer. I got a call from my wife, and she's leaving me. One of you sickos planted a notebook in the library, don't you think I can see that? You're all off your rockers. I mean, how do I even know those pages weren't blank? This guy just made all that up, luring me into your *trap*, and you know what? It ain't working, you lunatics. Wherever you've hidden Mr. Fisher, whatever you've *done* to him, don't worry, when I get back with the police, you can tell them, because I'm getting the fuck out of here. Oh, and if you try and stop me? It won't end well for any of you."

"Try." Peter said. Henry and Donald looked to him. "Tell them to get here as soon as they can, because all the phone lines are down. We have no cell phones, either, Fisher made sure of that. And just so you know, driving to town takes a half hour, so if you're to walk it in this weather . . . Well, be my guest."

"I will."

Andrew charged from the room, elbowing Peter aside, and Donny shot Peter a questioning look. *Well, kid? What are we gonna do?*

"Andrew, wait!"

Peter ran to the man and narrowly avoided getting his third blow in two days. Andrew's muscular arm swung but Peter expected it.

You don't take two punches in a day and not learn something.

He ducked as Andrew's knuckles cracked off the doorframe with a dull whack. Andrew balked, cradling his hand.

"You let me go, y'hear?"

"Sure," Peter said. "But help me get Walter back inside the house first. Please. He's as confused as the rest of us, okay? He'll freeze to death out there in his pajamas. As far as I know, you're in control here now that Fisher's absent. You can't call the police if one of your patients froze to death while in *your* care, now can you?"

Andrew's face fell sober. Peter didn't know what to expect, and didn't know what to do. Henry, with his old age, needed Donald by him because they couldn't be left alone, not with Phobos stalking about. Peter was going after Andrew. The large man wanted to leave, but they needed as much help as they could get to defeat Phobos, and this seemed to be the only option of slowing the man down while Peter came up with a better solution. The idea of somehow capturing Phobos, with Andrew to help them, seemed the only next step on the board. Check and mate. They *needed* Andrew's help.

"Please, Andrew," Peter said. "You need to help me get him back inside, keep him from harming himself, or someone else. Put him to bed, maybe? You've got some medication we can use to sedate him, don't you? There's got to be some in this place."

"We've got nothing here, Jerry said Dawson ran an organic detox." Andrew looked to the three of them and took a deep breath. "*I'll* get him inside, you hear me? *You* stay inside and don't move."

I can't let him do that, Peter thought. He didn't like Andrew, but letting him outside with Phobos? He couldn't live with himself if something happened. Sure, the man had tried to punch him, but it wasn't his fault. Peter would have done the same. Andrew had only tried to be rational.

"Andrew, wait. Hold on."

The large man left. Peter ran after, but Andrew was quicker, getting the door open and hopping the front steps in one stride. Then he took off straight ahead; down the yard and towards town. Peter stood on the porch, and watched him go.

"You fucking coward!" he shouted. "Get back here!"

Snow kicked up from Andrew's boots, leaving two jagged trenches in the white as his breath steamed away like a coal train. Then Donald and Henry appeared beside Peter, their eyes wide.

"Fucker made a *break* for it?" Donald asked. "Runnin' away?"

"Yeah, he did, Donny. Look, you stay here with Henry in case Jerry or Paul come back, all right?

"What are you going to do?" Henry asked.

"Just wait here."

Peter descended the porch steps, slipping on the ice. The snow swallowed his boots, the air stinging his lungs. He looked to the left of the house for any signs of Walter's footprints, trying to track the man, but saw none. He rounded the corner of the house, and froze. Before him, Walter levitated.

The deadman's legs dangled beneath his body, at least two inches above the ground. His feet hung, pointed down, as Walter glided with a grin splitting his face. He cast a look in Peter's direction before shooting off towards Andrew.

"Andrew!" Peter heard himself shout. "Andrew, run!"

Peter couldn't help the man now. Phobos could catch him in a snap, like a snake hunting prey; toying with it. Peter could only shout.

"Shit!"

He barged through the snow, lifting his legs almost to his stomach. Climbing the porch, he stood next to Donald and Henry, feeling safer with them than out in the dark, but not by much.

"Oh my God . . ."

The three watched in horror as their dead friend floated

towards Andrew. The orderly tripped and fell, getting to his feet and continuing with what had to be the last of his energy. Peter's stomach fell as he realized the deadman was indeed only toying with Andrew.

"Like a cat on a cornered mouse," Peter whispered.

"Poor fuck," Donald said. "He's got him . . . Done for."

The floating corpse sped up with frightening speed, gained on Andrew just as the he reached the fence at the bottom of the yard. He slammed into him, sending them both sprawling to the snow. Then Walter sat on Andrew's back, his bloated stomach jiggling. He grabbed hold of the frightened man's shoulders and slammed his head into the frosty powder. Andrew screamed, his voice muffled.

Walter cackled. "Are you watching, you ugly things? *Are you watching*?"

He brought Andrew's head up in an awkward angle by clutching his chin in both hands. The man's spine arched, and Phobos kept pulling. Peter yelled for him to stop it, but he knew it was useless. Phobos kept yanking, his weight pressing the man's back as Andrew's spine continued to bend, his face red and twisted.

"Stop!" Peter shouted.

Phobos let Andrew drop, the man panting for breath. On the porch, Henry moaned.

Then Phobos turned, facing the three of them while sitting on Andrew's back.

"Listen to this, boys. The feel good hit of the summer."

A sharp snap echoed across the yard. Crows cawed in response and Henry yelped.

Phobos dropped Andrew's broken leg to the snow, then lifted the other one. A second snap cracked out.

The large man let out an agonizing wail, his voice muffled and strained before Phobos stood, stumbling about, laughing. He wiped his hands together, the snow coating his bare back and shoulders. Then he raised his head to the three of his, his glasses crooked.

"Ta-da!"

He raised his arms like a child finishing a particularly good magic trick. Behind him, Andrew sobbed into the snow.

"He's fucking insane," Donald said. "I mean . . . What the fuck?"

Phobos wagged Walter's lifeless finger at them. "Oh now, now. Don't spoil this, my lovelies. Watch my next trick very carefully..."

He fell to his knees and slogged towards Andrew's twitching body. Then he buried his face into the back of the large man's neck. Andrew let out an ear splitting howl.

Donald jumped from foot to foot, his eyes wide. "He's fucking eating him alive!"

"Inside the house," Peter ordered. "Now!"

Donald led the way. Once in, Peter slammed the door shut and found a chain bolt. He slid it across with shaking fingers.

"The grandfather clock," Peter said. "We need to get this door secured. We can't let that thing inside."

"You two get that," Henry said, his voice unstable. "I'll see what I can find to board up the windows and back door."

Peter and Donald made for the large oak clock without a word between them, Henry rushing for the kitchen.

Donald looked to him. "Can you believe it? A moving fog, my head could take, all right? But a dead dude getting up and eating somebody alive? What the hell is this? A fuckin' zombie movie?"

Peter didn't respond. His stomach sloshed in waves of nausea. Outside, if he strained, he could hear Andrew weeping. Faint, but there.

"Come on," he said, rubbing his hands together. "On the count of three. One, two . . ."

They grasped the base of the clock, their arms straining. With some effort, they managed to skid it across the polished floor to the front door, leaving two long trailing scrapes in the hardwood.

"Here's good," Peter said, and dropped the clock. It clanged down with a hollow ringing.

Walter's voice came from beyond the bolted door. "Why, is that the dinner bell I hear?" his voice repeated around the empty house. "I'm mighty hungry, fellas. Been a long time since I had a good meal."

Peter's flesh crawled. He looked to Donald who looked ready

to vomit. "He's tryin' to eat us? He's *actually* gonna eat us?"

Henry returned, jogging across the hallway. "Did you hear that? What he just said?"

Peter avoided the question. "Did you find anything in the kitchen to board the place up?"

"No. Not unless we pull apart the table. But I had another idea."

"Oh?"

"The barn, Peter. The planks, the hammer, the nails. The whole lot is out there."

"You're right. But that won't do us any good tonight. You've seen the speed he moves at."

"Shit."

"Why do you think he didn't take Andrew's body over Walter's?" Donald asked. "Why don't he switch? That Andrew guy's is in better shape."

"Because the only way to kill Andrew was with his bare hands. Or teeth. And that's a messy job. Besides, he has three more of us right here, all in better shape than Walter. He's got a selection. And doing that little act right in front of us got us very frightened, weakened us. He'll be able to get inside our heads better, make us take our own lives."

"Sure," Donald said. He swallowed and gave a chuckle. "Or maybe we just taste better when we're scared. And in that case, I'm as tender as a gourmet fuckin' steak."

"Come on," Peter said. "I have something in mind. Let's gather more books from the library, take them to the living room and see what we can find. There's got to be something useful."

Back in the living room, they dumped another fifteen books to their pile and Donald made for the kitchen. He returned pulling the breakfast table behind him.

"Hold the fuckin' door open, kid. Gonna rip this thing to shreds. Light us up a fire."

Donald had the table apart in a matter of minutes. He started by setting the table against the wall and kicking through, splintering it to pieces. With the table in two, he worked the rest with his bare hands.

"Donny," Peter said, watching the act with interest. "You

seemed well adjusted to carrying Walter's body . . . Seeing you rip that table apart, I can't help but ask, you ever kill someone? Where did you come from?"

Donald stopped and wiped his forehead. "From Jersey, kid, that's about it. Nothin' out of the usual. Just had a life with tales to make a grown man weep, you know what I'm sayin'? But yeah, I've killed *two* men, if you've just gotta know. One was some sick fuck banging my wife while I was inside. Went in on possession, only served half my time. The missus wasn't expecting that. Had some fuckin' cunt of a neighbor over most every night stickin' her. Can't even remember what happened clearly." Donald gathered the four legs of the table in his arms and carried them to the fireplace. He began to build the fire as he continued. "Saw red, man. That's all I fuckin' know. Started punchin' the bastard in the face. *Bam, bam, bam.* Caught him in one of my bathrobes, can you believe it? Sitting in *my* living room, watching *my* TV. Punched him until he stopped screaming. And that's all I know. Was in another world. But, I tell ya, I wasn't even coked up. If I'd had a few bumps, he'd be pulp. Now he wasn't much better, the way it was, but I probably would have kept slammin' his face for hours if I'd been jacked. I stopped when his eyes stopped focusin'. His fuckin' teeth were lyin' around like pieces of popcorn. Must have broke his skull in a million places. Cops were there before I knew it, pullin' me off."

He paused for thought with a shake of his head, then lit a wad of newspaper he'd put beneath the table legs in the fireplace. He spotted a bottle of lighter fluid on the mantle and squirted a liberal amount onto the wood. The fire danced an orange glow on his face.

"There," he said. "Table should keep us goin' for a while."

"Thanks, Donny," Peter said, still curious. "And the second man?"

"Prison. You don't need to have a very fuckin' broad imagination to wonder why I did that, new guy and all. Split his neck open with a broken plastic knife in the cafeteria."

"How long did you get for doing that?"

"No one saw nothin'. They knew who he was. Even the wardens were waiting for someone to do it. He was some fat-cat drug lord or something, well known on the streets, lotta manpower behind him. Nobody wanted to touch him."

"But you did?"

"I did. And no one saw me do it, you get me? If anything, that little stabby-stabby sped the process of me gettin' outta there. I was a fuckin' hero."

Donald's eyes seemed far away as he thought. Then he stood. "And if you think some bastard, supernatural or not, is going to end Donny Bove's life with his mouth, you got another thing comin'. He'll choke on my fuckin' bones at the least. He's fucked with the wrong dude. Now you just tell me what we need to do."

The request snapped Peter back into reality. He thought it over, something striking him as funny. Nothing to laugh out loud about, but still, something interesting. Back in the days of *Throttle*, the other members would always wait for him to make the big decisions, just as Donald and Henry were now. Robby and Bill never scheduled rehearsals, never booked a recording session, never signed a contract without Peter doing so first. They left those jobs to him, making him their *leader*. And it went back even further. Peter remembered being a kid in his grandmother's place. Down the street there'd been a trailer park that would fill up during the Summer. On a few occasions, he'd had a handful of kids to play with for a while, other than Beth. They were nice kids, and together they played all week long. Video games, mess-wrestling, imaginary war missions, all the usual things that children do. But those kids had also asked Peter what it was they were going to do next, each and every day. Peter had never much thought about it. He fell into the role without question, because it was all he ever knew. He'd never had someone else try to take the reins. They followed by default, and Peter was left to lead. Whether he liked it or not.

"Well?" Henry asked. "What are we going to do?"

"We read through these books," Peter said. "We find something to help us."

From outside, Phobos laughed. "Little pigs, little pigs, *let me in . . .*"

CHAPTER TWELVE

"Anything?" Donald asked. "We need to speed this up, fellas. That sick fuck could be anywhere."

Peter lowered the book in his hands. He didn't know whether to say he'd found nothing, or that he'd found too much. Engraved on the pages were images of creatures unimaginable. On one page, more of those Lizard Men stood around an open cauldron, while on the next, a giant worm or leech took up the entire page that left Peter ill. After some more pages of text came a hairy, humanoid entity, giant claws swinging by its sides. After that, sea creatures. Another page showed what appeared to be a vampire with crooked, thin teeth jutting from its lips. Peter tried to control the tremors in his chest.

"You think these things *exist*?" He asked. "I mean, if Phobos is real, what about the rest of these? I mean, look at this one."

Peter held the book out to Donald.

"Jesus," the large man said. "Those fuckin' zombies?"

"If they exist, I want to die right now."

"Calm it, Peter," Henry said, his face buried in a book. He raised his head. "Keep searching for something useful."

Peter returned to the text, and not long after, found something. An ink spatter, not unlike a Rorschach test. The word *Phobos* had been repeatedly underlined with a red pen.

"Think I've got something," he mumbled. "The text is in another language, same as the rest, but Jerry or Harris made some long hand notes on the side. Check it out."

He passed the book to Henry who scanned it while Donald peered over his shoulder. "Leave it with me," Henry said, not taking his eyes from the page. "I think I've got something else, too. I don't know what it is just yet, but it's nagging me. Look."

Henry held up the other book and Peter squinted at a crude drawing of the sea. Next to it, within the foreign text, the word *Phobos* repeated over and over, along with illustrations of cadavers in various stages of decomposition. "There's a connection between these pages," Henry said. "Like solving a puzzle. Give me more time with it."

Peter nodded. "We need to find this basement. You think Jerry's got any food or water? A toilet?"

"Who gives a shit," Donald said. "Let the fucker starve."

"What I mean is, he'll have to come up at some point."

"I'm more concerned about the clock in front of the door," Donald said. "Took two of us to lift it, but what if he's got some sort of super-human strength or some shit?"

A heavy crash from the hallway answered the man's question.

"Come on!"

Peter dashed to the hallway, Henry and Donald close behind. His breath caught in his throat. "He knocked it over . . ."

The clock lay in shards on the hardwood, snow bellowing in from the open door. Peter saw no sign of Walter.

Phobos, He corrected himself. *Not Walter. Not anymore. It's Phobos.*

Henry swallowed, his eyes glistening. "He's playing with us. Like a damn animal playing with its food. He's trying to frighten us."

"You think he's here in the house?" Donald whispered. Peter knew why the man kept his voice down. It felt wrong to speak aloud, as if the walls had ears. The safety of the living room didn't exist out here. Now they stood in the territory of a wild beast that could strike at any second.

A window smashed.

"We gotta stop that freak from getting in," Donald said, "Come on!" He rushed to the television room, Peter and Henry following close behind. Donald elbowed the door and fell inside. "Jesus Christ!" He swung out his arm and hit Peter in the chest, stopping him.

Phobos swung his arms about on the shattered window frame, raking his flesh over shards of glass. The glistening spikes, like jagged teeth, tore his arms to ribbons as dark crimson dribbled down the inner wall.

Phobos giggled. "It tickles, did you know that? How utterly

delightful to feel again."

The creature continued sawing his arms, back and forth, back and forth. A swinging vein caught on a sharp piece and severed, spraying blood onto the wall.

"Make some room, boys. I'm comin' in."

Peter fought to stay grounded. He wanted to run, make a break just as Andrew did.

"You fuckin' creep," Donald spat. "You sick fuckin' freak."

He tossed a lamp from a nearby tabletop and it shattered on the deadman's bald spot.

Phobos raised his head. "Well, that wasn't very nice of you. I'll do you slow for that, Donald Bove."

"Try it, you sick fuck."

Although Donald put up a strong act, Peter noticed none of them were stepping inside the room. They weren't running, either.

Phobos shook his head, spilling off the remnants of the lamp. "Up we go, boys!"

Then the deadman jumped, impaling his large stomach on the window cavity. He lay half in, half out, legs kicking in a frenzy. Peter's stomach flipped as the shards bit their way into the fat of their dead friend's belly. Phobos wheezed, continuing to slither inside. He gave a grunt as he tipped, crashing to the pool of crimson and glass on the carpet. His shredded stomach jiggled, the deep cuts beginning to open. He sat like a baby, legs spread.

"Look at this," he said, "Such thin lines . . . Gonna open as wide as a mouth any moment now, don't you think?"

The three men stood frozen by the door, silent with shock.

"Could speed it along, huh? That might help."

Henry moaned as Phobos slid a hand inside one of the slices, the skin resisting at first, but with a wiggle, it popped right through. All the way to the wrist.

"Ah . . . The sting's damn good, you know that? *So good* . . . You don't know how lucky you have it . . . Better run, boys . . ."

Peter grabbed Henry and Donald by their shirts and pulled them from the room. They sped by the shattered clock and into the living room. Peter slammed the door shut and rammed his shoulder against it. Donald and Henry did the same. The three of them pressed their weight to the frame, listening for any sign of their dead friend. It didn't take long.

Footsteps clomped along the hallway, Walter's bare feet smacking the hardwood, making the sound louder on purpose.

"I wonder where you've gone?" Walter's announced. "You were only here a second ago, how strange . . . It's almost as if you just disappeared into thin air, isn't it?"

Henry whimpered and Peter shushed him.

"You wouldn't happen to be inside, oh, I don't know, say, the kitchen?"

Phobos waited for a response. "Okay. How about the living room then? How. About. The living room?"

Donald shot Peter a wide-eyed look, sweat beading down his forehead. Peter closed his eyes, his heart punching his chest. What he would give for a damn swig of whiskey at this moment.

"I guess I'll just try the living room, then. Seems a good a place as any."

"Shit," Donald whined. He shook his head back and forth. Outside, Walter's footsteps sped up as the deadman charged the door.

Peter braced, anticipating the smack. The footsteps shook the floor, like an elephant charging—and then stopped short of the door. Peter's squeezed his eyes shut, waiting. He gritted his teeth.

Phobos' breathing came fast and heavy just beyond the frame, inches away. Peter's skin crawled. He swallowed, his throat clicking in the silence.

The deadman ran his fingernails down the other side of the door at a steady pace, the rumble-like scratch seeming to last a lifetime and reminding Peter of faraway thunder.

"Come on, fellas . . . Give it up, will ya?"

He brought his hand back up and scraped his nails a second time. "It's your pal Walter . . . You know I'm not safe by myself out here. You know I need someone to look after me . . . That wasn't very friendly of you to leave me outside in the snow. Half naked of all things. My poor little pecker froze right off."

Peter could hear the deadman trying to keep the laugher from his voice. "I might have a good bit of blubber on me, but that wouldn't keep me alive out there for a whole night, now would it? Nope." The word smacked on his lips. "No, no, no way. See, that wasn't very *friendly*... Not friendly at all."

"Go away," Donald whispered. "Just go the fuck away, you fuck. Go away . . ."

Phobos slammed the door with a fist, making the three of them shout. "Ah fuck it," he said. "Done playin'."

The deadman's hand smashed through the wood, wrapping around Peter's shoulder. He tried to pull away but the fist felt like a vise.

"Shit!"

Peter beat at the hand, wincing at the cold, slimy texture.

Like an icy slug, he thought. *Oh, Jesus . . .*

"Help me!"

Phobos roared with laugher, his grip tightening. "You scared, you fuckin' alco? *You scared?*"

Donald raced to the fire place and came back with a leg of the table. "You sick fuck!" he yelled, raising the leg like a spear. He brought the splintered end down hard on the dead hand, missing Peter's shoulder by inches. Phobos wailed.

"You do that *so* good, Don! Oh! Do it again, baby!"

Cold blood trickled down Peter from the wound, staining his shirt and filling his nose with a metallic scent. Then Phobos released his grip.

Peter stumbled from the door, gasping and wiping the blood from his chest. He stood by the other two, watching the door.

It's going to burst open at any second, I just know it . . .

But instead, Phobos shoved his eye to the hole where his hand had been. The pupil danced around until it found them, the skin around his eye wrinkling as he smiled.

"Peek-a-boo," he said. "I seeeee you."

Nobody moved.

"You know, if I wanted to, I could take this door down within a matter of seconds, right? And that terrifies you, doesn't it? I could take this door down and have you all cornered. I could strip away the flesh from your bones and make a three-course meal. Peter for starters, Randolph for a main, and fatty Bove for a dessert. He'd be the sweetest. How tasty, how . . . *delicious.*

Especially Mr. Chub-chub Bove . . . Donald, Donny, Don, don't you agree, Mr. Plump? My, what juicy thighs you have. My mouth's watering already."

Rage bubbled inside Peter as an idea struck. His lips moved by their own accord. "But you'd ruin our bodies doing that, wouldn't you? You won't do that!"

Silence. Henry and Donald threw each other a worried glance.

"You're right," Peter said. "Here we are, you sick fuck, we're cornered. Come and get us. Strip our flesh from our bones, as you put it. Come on."

Phobos' eye relaxed, the wrinkles disappearing. No longer smiling, now the monster glared.

"That's right, asshole. You need us in good condition. You need us to feel frightened so you can worm away at our heads, to get inside and make us do the dead. What's the best case scenario for you, huh? Heart attack? At least it'll leave the body in good shape. We know who you are, *Phobos*."

The creature flinched.

Peter smiled. "You didn't think we had a clue, did you? Thought we saw our dead friend and would freak the fuck out. Nah, we know exactly who you are." Peter pocketed his hands. They shook. He didn't want the monster to see. He licked at his dry lips and continued. "You're not even human. You're from somewhere else, somewhere you don't want to be. See, we're one step ahead of you . . . *And you don't scare us.*"

Phobos hissed, the noise not unlike a leaf-clogged drainpipe. "*You lie, little one . . . I see you shake . . . You* fear *me . . .*"

Peter kept his voice collected. "No. I don't."

Phobos watched them silently for a moment before the eye disappeared from the hole in the door. No footsteps came, no sounds whatsoever, but somehow, Peter knew the monster had gone. A palpable pressure lifted.

Looking to Peter, Henry whispered, "How did you do that?"

Peter exhaled a shaking breath, the adrenaline leaving his body. "I was just all out of ideas . . ."

Donald fell to the couch with a sigh and rubbed at his temples. His colorless skin glistened with a layer of fresh sweat.

He looked in danger of passing out.

"Do anything for a fuckin' cigarette right now. Sweet Jesus…"

"Henry," Peter said. "Sit down, too. You don't look so good."

He led Henry to the couch and sat him down before throwing one of the other table legs onto the fire. It'd dipped to embers now but still glowed.

"He was toying with us," Peter said, watching a flame lick the wood. "That's what he was doing."

"But it don't make us taste better," Donald said. "Just trying to weasel inside our heads and make us swallow a bunch of pills or somethin'. Something that'll leave us intact, right?"

"Right. The more we're afraid, the easier it gets for him to crawl around inside. Once he's in, he can use whatever's lying around in there against us. We saw it happen with Walter, and with Jamie. We even saw it happen with you, Henry. With your son. And to me."

Henry nodded.

"He could burrow further with the more he knows. Walter was terrified so he was easy pickings, that's what Jerry was talking about in his journal. It clicked with me when I looked into that bastard's eye through the door. He was trying to make us afraid . . . It all fell into place. It's funny . . ."

"What's funny?" Henry asked.

"That he did the same thing as Jerry Fisher and Harris Dawson. Ancient deity or not, he underestimated us."

"How so?"

Peter chuckled. "Because we've got nothing to lose, man. Fuck, I mean, think about it. We're at the end of our ropes. They forgot to take that into consideration. Jerry and Harris picked a rehab center as a cover scheme because they saw us as weak, vulnerable… Easy pickings. They were right, to an extent. We are weak in some ways. But back us in a corner and there's no telling what'll happen . . ."

Donald grinned. "Never underestimate a man who's got nothin' to fuckin' lose."

"Damn right."

CHAPTER THIRTEEN

"Peter, you can't go out there."

Henry's grip tightened on Peter's arm. "It's suicide. You saw what he did to Andrew."

Peter's hand slipped from the door handle. "He got to Andrew only because Andrew was afraid. He ran from us, Henry, you saw that. He fears us not being afraid. Without that, he's got nothing. Let me go."

"Peter, please—"

"Look." Peter licked at his lips. "We've got a chance at trying something here, otherwise we're just waiting to die. If I go out there, show him I'm not afraid, we might stand a chance at beating him."

"And what if it doesn't work?"

"There's only one way to find out."

From the couch, Donald called out. "Let the kid go, Henry. He's right. We need to do something."

Henry shook his head in disbelief. "And why don't you go, Don? Huh?"

"I've got a little girl at home that I'm here to clean myself up for." He ran a hand through his hair. "You wanna think of me as a chickenshit? You go right ahead and do that, but I can't die here. I need to see her again . . . The kid's got a plan. Shit, it could be our secret weapon. You're like, armored or some shit when you're not afraid. That thing can't get inside your head."

Henry stepped aside. "I think this is a bad idea, Peter. But if you really believe it'll work . . ."

"I do," Peter said. "I have to. There's a kid on the way that I need to get out of here for. I need to do this."

"Be safe."

Peter took a deep breath before opening the door and stepping into the hallway. Deep down, he felt his theory was correct. But what if it wasn't? What if he'd done the very thing Phobos had and underestimated the beast?

Only one way to find out, Peter thought.

Peter sidestepped the shattered clock and stepped onto the front porch. Before him, dancing snowflakes peppered the air while a crescent moon loomed overhead. The snow in the yard appeared more blue than white. Peter scanned for the creature.

Where are you . . . Come on . . .

Peter's heart jumped as he spotted Phobos. Out near the point Andrew met his gruesome end, the deadman hovered, Walter's dirt covered feet dangling. His skin looked gray in the moonlight, the cuts and welts sticking out in high contrast. His mouth hung open.

"*Peter . . .*"

Peter's breath shook as took a step forward, his hands clenched into tight fists. "I'm done playing this game, Phobos. You're not going to win."

"*But I'm not done with you . . .*"

The words made Peter want to vomit, but he pressed on. "What can you tell me that I don't already know, huh? That I'm a leech? A burden? That I won't make a good father? I already know that. I've accepted that . . . You hold no power over me."

Walter's lips curled into a smile. "*Oh, but I do, Peter Laughlin. I do . . . Wait and see.*"

Peter's chest lurched. He wanted to run, wanted to go back inside and find another plan. But deep down, he knew he had to see this through. He took another step forward. "I'm not afraid of you!"

Phobos hissed, a noise like a kettle over-boiling. He threw his hands in front of his face, white palms facing outward. "*Vile thing!*" he screamed. "*You will fear me!*"

Then Walter's body fell to the snow, thumping beside Andrew's corpse like a used-up rag doll. Snowflakes began covering it instantly.

An involuntary sound escaped Peter's lips. Did he do it? Had he defeated Phobos so *easy*?

"No . . . Please . . ."

From Walter's crumpled body, a black fog oozed, curled upward and growing.

There you are, Peter thought, his hair standing on end. *There's the real you . . .*

He back-stepped into the house, not able to tear his eyes from the sight. An arm clutched his shoulder.

"Peter," Henry said. "We watched from the window."

Peter swallowed, fighting back the urge to vomit. "Let's get back into the living room. He's out of Walter and in the air. I . . . I did something."

"I know. Come on."

They sat around the fire, Donald using the final two table legs to keep it ablaze. Peter watched the flames twist and dance, the standoff against Phobos playing over and over in his mind.

"Kid," Donald said, his voice snapping Peter back to reality. "I think you weakened it. Can't get us if we're not afraid. You were brave."

Peter didn't have a response. The sight of Phobos curling away from Walter's corpse left him dazed. Just what in God's name were they up against?

"Why doesn't he leave us alone?" Donald asked. "I mean, there's gotta be hundreds of people in town. Why doesn't he leave?"

"Maybe because he can't," Peter said, his voice a monotone.

"Why not?"

"I know as much as you do, Donny."

Henry sighed. "We have to be strong and not let him inside our heads, that's the priority. If we find the basement, we can find Fisher and force him to stop this thing . . . If he can. If that fails, there's *got* to be something in one of these books to help us." He swiped one of the volumes from the floor and flicked though the pages. "I'm still listening, just want to get a head start."

"We're sure there ain't no way outta here?" Donald asked. His skin looked the color of curdled milk.

"Road's no use," Peter said. "No keys for the bus even if it was. Besides, getting past that *thing* would be impossible."

"What if we started hollerin' and screamin'? Someone would hear us, right?"

"We've got a plan," Henry said, looking up from his book. "What's getting at you, Don?"

"I need to tell you guys somethin'." Donald leaned on the mantelpiece. "That thing took the shape as an ice cream man for

Walter, right? Because Walt told that bastard Fisher all about his childhood. Then it showed *you* your son, and imitated *your* gramma, scared the crap outta all you. Because Fisher made you tell him about your fears, right? Well, I told Fisher some stuff, too, you know. Back when I had my session."

Peter lowered himself to the couch, anticipating the blow. "What did you tell him about?"

"Spiders, man. Freak me the fuck out. My momma, God bless that lady's soul, she was *terrified* of 'em. Terrified. Used to shriek the damn house down if a tiny guy, not even the size of a nickel, would come scramblin' across the floor. She'd be up on the table fast, man. Screamin' *get the bastard, get it, get it*! So, me or my brother'd have to fetch the broomstick, right? Smack the fuck. She'd have to see us whack it, too, or she wouldn't come down. Would stay up there askin' *is it gone, is it gone*? Yeah, ma, it's gone, I'd say, and then she'd come down, but shakin', man, shakin'. I never minded spiders until I got my first place, and I don't know, maybe it was from watching her react like that, you know? Started me doin' the same. Couldn't help it, man! Saw those little legs scurrying and my skin would *crawl*. I'd start to make noises, you know, involuntary? And I'd just start *shakin'*. I'd always go kill the fuck, but it would take me forever. And, man, if the thing was big? Like, even just a little big? I'm done for. *Done for*, man. Can't take it."

"Shit."

"Huh? What?" Donald said. Peter noticed sweat stains on the man's armpits. "You think there's gonna be a giant fuckin' spider crashin' through that door? Don't say that man, don't say that."

"Let's just change the subject."

"Ah, fuck." Donald rubbed at his forehead. "You know, when you were passed out, Henry told me you were a musician, kid. That true?"

Peter smiled. " *Was* a musician . . . That's a slap to the face to say, but I it's true. Haven't done anything creative in a long time. Was my whole life up until the band broke up. That's a hard thing to admit, man. I still *think* of myself as a musician, but I guess I'm not anymore . . . We were called *Throttle*. The band. Three-piece rock setup."

"Never hearda ya."

Peter laughed. "Yeah, didn't think so. We did all right. *Better* than all right, actually. Did at least one European tour a year by the time we broke up, that was our schedule. We weren't headliners, but we had good special guest slots. Managed to get on a lot of the European festival circuits with bigger bands, too."

"So what happened?"

"The guys couldn't commit." Peter found it odd to be talking about the band in such a strange situation, but found himself continuing nonetheless. "Robbie, the drummer, that guy was a family man at heart. I could tell from the start. Sometimes you can just look at a man and know. Bill, my bass player, he always saw himself as a hired hand. I was the writer, the leader, the front man. I was a road dog. I could stay on tour and never come home, if that's what it took. I guess it's because I had nothing to come back to."

Peter swallowed down a lump in his throat. "But I have something to get back to now. You know, the idea of spending time with Beth makes my chest hurt. Just watching movies, planting a garden, cooking good food . . . Anything. Just being together. I have to get out of here. We've got a kid on the way."

Henry's voice snapped Peter out of his thoughts. "I've got something."

Peter and Donald looked to him.

"It looks like the others," Henry said. "All bizarre pictures and Latin-like text, but look at this." He held up the page, showing a splash of black ink. Opposite the odd splatter, someone had circled paragraphs of the text.

Donald's brow creased. "So? What about it?"

"It says *Phobos* over and over. See? It's got to be something."

"A summoning spell?" Peter guessed.

"Or a banishing one," Henry said. "That's what I'm thinking."

Peter found himself smiling. "God, we can only hope."

"The things I'd do for a fuckin' cigarette right now," Donald said. "I know it's not a good time, but Jesus, I can't stop thinkin' about it."

Peter felt the same. His head throbbed from lack of nicotine. He let out a slow breath, relieving some of the tension inside him . . . and let it back in slowly.

"You know, in a roundabout way, Fisher did get us clean."

"Oh, thank fuck for that," Donald said, slapping his hands down. "At least if I fuckin' die, I'll die clean and sober, what use that'll be, I mean—"

A muffled thump came from upstairs. The three men stared at the ceiling. A floorboard creaked, followed by another.

"Guys," Donald whispered. "My head's reelin' without my coke, but please say that you heard that, too."

"I heard it," Peter said, watching the roof. He knew staring at the ceiling wouldn't do any good, but he couldn't look away. "Somebody moved up there."

"Jerry?" Henry asked. "Or Paul?"

"Gotta be," Donald said. "And if it's Fisher, there's only one way out of here and that's down the stairs. As long as I'm breathin', he's not making it out the door. He's giving us answers."

Tap-tap-tap-tap.

Something scuttled overhead, moving from one side of the room to the other.

"What the hell *is* that?" Donald asked, his voice shaking. "Guys, what the hell is that?"

Henry's face scrunched in confusion. "Sounded like somebody falling around up there . . ."

They listened. A single floorboard groaned.

Donald balled his fists. "Fuck it. I'm done with this shit, man."

"Don, wait." Peter grabbed for the man's arm but missed, then Donald opened the door.

"Oh, jumpin' Jesus . . ."

Peter grunted as Donald fell back into him, forcing his way back into the room. "Shut that fuckin' door, shut it."

"What? What is it?" Peter squinted into the darkness, and fought the urge to scream.

Spider webs covered the hallway.

From the chandelier, a large white web connected to the landing of the second floor, glistening in the light of the living room. To Peter, it looked as thick as rope. A thin, silky coating caked every visible surface, mummifying the shattered clock on the floor. On the second floor, something caught Peter's attention. He squinted.

"What in God's name is that?"

His stomach fell as his vision cleared. A series of circular eyes, four in a row, stared back. Not from multiple creatures, Peter noticed, but from a single beast. Two large eyes flanked two small ones, all surrounded by coarse, black hair. Whatever the eyes belonged to had to be gargantuan.

"You see it?" Henry whispered. Peter hadn't noticed him step up to his side. "Up there. You see it?"

Peter nodded. "Hard to miss. It's watching us."

"W-what?" Donald asked from behind. "What's fuckin' watchin' us?"

"Calm it, Don."

"Don't say it's one of those fuckin' *things*, don't. Come on. A huge one?"

Peter stared at him. "You know it is and you need to keep calm. It wants you to be afraid, you know this."

"Close the fuckin' door!"

Donald barged past and shoved the door closed, making it shake in its frame. He stalked to the middle of the room, looking back on the door as if it was a feral animal. "It's gonna come down, man. I just know it's gonna come get me."

Then the creature scurried down the staircase. The floorboards moaned in protest. Peter chanced a glance through the hole in the door.

"It's coming!" he said. "Get back!"

The spider raised to its hind legs, coming to the height of the doorframe and exposing a black, waxy underbelly. Its legs twitched and curled, coarse hair glistening, as shining mandibles clicked. Then it crashed down.

Peter dived to the side as the door ripped free of its hinges and skidded across the hardwood. The large spider slapped down, its fleshy hind elevated and its head lowered. Its deep, dark eyes closed at different rates.

Peter sprawled over the couch, squatting to hide. The spider hissed before spitting a wad of silky web in his direction. The web smacked the wall before dribbling down like mucus. Peter shifted to avoid it landing on him.

He heard the creature scuttled.

"Help me!"

Donald backed towards the window, his wide eyes fixed upon the monstrosity. It stalked towards him, cornering him. The large man's mouth moved, but no words came, only a series of shaking whines. Peter's chest lurched as a wet spot blossomed on Donald's pants. The man's bladder had let go.

"Get away from him!"

Peter shot for the beast, shouting at the top of his voice. He clasped his hands and brought them over his head, swinging down as hard as he could on the monster's hind. The hit connected with a dull thump, the creature's greasy hair wetting his fists. Peter grabbed the hair and pulled away a fistful. The monster hissed before spinning to face him, knocking a wall table to the floor. Peter froze, coming face to face with the giant spider.

Four large, globe-like eyes reflected the room. Peter saw his own face in them, bug-eyed and multiplied. The creature took a step forward, the waxy tips of its mandibles clicking.

It's going to bite me . . .

Then Peter saw something else in the creature's four eyes. Behind four terrified Peters, came four Henry Randolphs, carrying four table legs.

"Henry, stay back!"

The spider hissed, raising its hind. Peter threw himself to the wall just as another spray of web jetted forth.

Henry moved quick. The old man ducked, avoiding the web by inches. He picked up speed and held the table leg like a baseball bat, then he yelled and swung. The leg cut the air with a whoosh, connecting with the creature's far right eye. A sickening splatter followed. The monster screeched, raising its front legs in defense, trying to take the old man down. But once again, Henry moved fast. He jabbed at the damaged eye, the table leg bursting through and stuck in place like Arthur's sword from the stone.

Henry fell back, looking both surprised and amazed at his actions.

The creatures eye sizzled and spat. Tendrils of smoke drifted from the wound, then the spider scrambled for the door, shooting past Peter with frightening speed. It screeched as it lost balance and cracked its head on the doorframe before scuttling into the hallway, its legs tapping the hardwood like amplified raindrops. Then the tapping stopped, cutting off in mid stride.

"It's gone?" Henry asked.

"Sounds like it just . . . Disappeared . . . Donald!"

Peter jogged to the man as he crumpled, his legs giving out. Donald thumped the floor hard enough to make Peter wince, his expression blank and his skin caked in sweat.

"Damn spider, man," he spoke, his voice a monotone. "Sonofabitch knew how to get me. Knew it would scare the shit outta me. And it did, kid."

"We got rid of him," Henry said. He kneeled beside Donald. "It's gone. We're all right now."

"No man, we ain't. That bastard's gonna pick us off one by one, don't think it won't. That was just the fuckin' beginnin'. Wanted to scare me? Fuckin' right it did. And I shit myself." Over Henry's shoulder, he gave Peter a cold stare. "Not kiddin', kid. Smell that? I shit my pants. You think that's funny, you try facing down somethin' straight outta your nightmares and see how you do."

"I never said it was funny, Donald."

And nor did Peter find it funny. He knew all too well how it felt to shit your pants and not be aware of it. Only in his case, it had been on account of a bad night of boozing. At least Donald's experience had some kind of dignity to it. Peter had no excuse.

A clatter rang out from the kitchen.

"What the fuck is happening now?" Donald asked.

Peter frowned. "Sounded like a pot falling."

Then came a groan, echoing through the hall.

"Someone's out there," Peter said. He stood and made for the door. "Sounds hurt."

"Peter," Henry called. "Wait, don't go out alone."

Peter eased towards the hallway, squinting through the gap where the door'd once stood.

". . . What the . . ."

He saw no sign of the injured spider. The cobwebs had disappeared. Everything looked just as it had before the attack. But something moved in the darkness.

CHAPTER FOURTEEN

"Move aside, Henry, coming through."

"Paul?" Henry sidestepped from the doorway as Peter carried Paul into the room. A gash lined the man's forehead, dribbling down his face. Blood pooled in his swollen left eye socket and his puffed lips were cracked and dry. Dark brown stains caked his white uniform. As Peter jogged for the couch, Paul moaned with each step.

"Clear the way, come on, give me a hand."

Henry swiped the books from the couch and stepped aside as Peter dropped the man to the cushions. Paul squeezed his eyes shut, breathing heavily through his nose. Peter guessed that the rest of the man's body to be in as bad a condition as his face.

"What happened?" Henry asked.

Peter rubbed at his forehead. "He was in the hallway like this, stumbling around the place. Collapsed on me. Paul? *Paul*, can you hear me?"

As Paul opened his mouth, Peter saw gaps where teeth should be "Fisher . . ." The orderly's words slurred, his voice thick. He took a clogged breath and winced. "Lost his mind . . . Tried to kill me . . . "

Peter's nostrils flared. He wanted to find Fisher, right now. "Where is he, Paul?"

Paul's eyes widened, as if waking from a bad dream. He fixed Peter a frightened stare. "I had no idea what he was up to, man. Honest. Swear to God, I just came here to work . . ." Tears spilled down his face. "You gotta believe me."

Peter looked to the other two. Henry looked lost for words, but Donald shuffled from the window, crossing the room with an awkward gait due to the mess in his pants. He peered down on Paul, his face flat.

"He's lyin'. Bastard knows exactly what's what. He's a fuckin' decoy, tryin' to weed us out. Jerry probably paid 'em extra to mess him up some. Ain't that right, Pauly? How much you get to look like you went a round with the champ?"

"Donny, relax."

Donald's nostrils flared at the remark and Peter drew back. He knew Donald wasn't thinking straight after the attack, but still, taking a punch off the man wasn't something Peter wanted to experience. To allow Donald near Paul right now wouldn't do anyone any favors, either. Peter eased between the two men, moving as subtle as possible.

"Paul," Peter said. "Tell us what happened."

"Crowbar . . . He's got a crowbar down there. In the basement. The smell . . . it's unbearable." He shook his head back and forth. "He locked me in with him. Started chanting in some weird language . . . I swear, that poor lady's body, it started moving."

"Shelly Matthews?" Peter asked, stunned. "You saw what happened to Shelly?"

"Her body moved, man . . . That kind of thing isn't supposed to happen."

Peter pressed on. "Did you take Jamie's body down there, too?"

"Yes," Paul said. It came out as *yash* from his swollen lips. "Fisher said he had a freezer. We'd leave the body there until an ambulance got up to retrieve it. I believed him . . . But when I started down the steps, he pushed me. I stumbled, landed on the floor. It's just dirt down there. A cellar. You wouldn't believe it if I told you . . ."

"Told us what, Paul?"

"The basement, it's hidden like something out of a movie. Disguised as a cupboard in the kitchen."

"This is ridiculous," Donald said. "The fuck kind of psychos are these people?"

Henry shook his head. "That's why we found no tracks in the snow. He never left the house."

"That poor lady's body was just muck, man," Paul said, his chest hitching. "Like a puddle of rancid meat, nothin' else. Jerry brought that kid down and told me to stay quiet. I couldn't breathe, that fall knocked me senseless. He put the boy on a table and did some sort of *ritual*. I swear, the kid's . . . The kid's corpse started to *spasm*. His bones started splitting, his skin all stretchy. Fisher laughed and laughed and I screamed like I've never screamed before."

"Does he have any other weapon down there besides the crowbar?" Peter asked.

"That's all I saw. He threatened to use it on me if I didn't shut it. That boy's body, man, all stretched out of shape and stuff . . ."

Donald snorted. "Phobos didn't fit into his new suit, eh? What's that Jerry said in his journal? Overeager."

"And how'd you get out?" Henry asked.

Paul croaked, tears spilling down his cheeks. "I just had to get away from that freak show . . . Made a run for it, but Jerry swung that crowbar out of nowhere. Managed to dodge the worse of it but he clipped me on the forehead. Then he caught hold of me and just started wailing me with the thing. I blocked my face but he banged up my ribs and arms real bad. I thought I was done for, but, praise Jesus, I caught it . . . Ripped it free and smacked him back in the face. Got him good, too. Think I banged out a couple of teeth, at least. Pried open the door of the cellar with the bar and managed to get up the stairs. I must have hurt him bad because he didn't chase me."

"I don't think it would be Fisher's smartest move to come up here," Peter said. "He knows we'd get him. You can relax here."

"Let 'em relax? Donald said. "I don't fuckin' trust him. You believin' him, Henry?"

The old man sighed. "Don, look at his face. See the damage? You think he'd do that to himself? Just to, what, infiltrate our group?"

"S'exactly what I'm sayin'."

"Don." Peter spoke slow, avoiding a confrontation. "I see where you're coming from, but I agree with Henry. Look at him. Listen to him. It checks out to me."

"Oh yeah? And what about this cellar, eh? Because we're obviously goin' down there, but when you take your first step and Jerry jumps out swingin', then what you gonna do? He pushes you down the rest of the steps and locks that door. You're stuck down there. And you're in much better shape than a heroin junkie and a dead kid. That fuckin' Phobos could get inside you easier than I could a hooker at midnight, am I right? Then he'd be back. And that's what Jerry Fisher wanted all along, isn't it? To bring this thing to life in our world? How fuckin' convenient. Nuh-uh. I ain't buyin' this fuck's story for a second."

Peter had to admit Donald had a point. Jerry Fisher and Harris Dawson had gone to extreme lengths to get the group here, after all, to use them as guinea pigs and cocoons for their Lord and Savior. They had the money and the resources, who's to say they couldn't hire a man who was willing to bruise himself up for a large chunk of cash?

"I tell you what," Peter said. "*Henry* and I will go check out the cellar. How about it, Don? You don' trust this man, so you keep an eye on him. Jerry can't take the both of us on at the same time. If Paul's telling the truth, we have him cornered. If Paul's lying, well then, we'll corner him. Somehow or other. And all the while, you can stay here and watch him. He's in no condition to make it very far. How does that sound?"

Donald thought it over, his face twitching. Leaving the man alone with Paul wasn't the best option, but Peter saw no other choice. After all, Donald had killed two men.

"Okay." Donald said at last. "That's what we'll do. You two go. I stay here."

"You sure?"

"You not?"

Peter considered, then nodded. "Henry, let's go."

From the couch, Paul cried out. Peter thought it sounded as authentic as it gets. No man could wail that way if they weren't feeling it.

"Keep alert," Henry said to Donald they left the room. "Shout if you need us."

Peter watched every inch of the hall as they passed, afraid of being caught unaware by the beast. Twice, he heard a board creak but Henry assured him it was just the house settling from the weather.

"Can you believe it?" Henry asked. "A *hidden* cellar . . . That's like something H.H. Homes would do."

"Who?"

"Never mind. Hey, stand back."

Henry eased open the kitchen swing door and stepped inside. "Looks clear," he whispered, and Peter followed. A row of white-doored cupboards sat below the sink, a sink Peter remembered washing a face cloth in not all too long ago while talking to a happy and smiling Paul.

"One of 'em's open," Peter said, getting to his knees and closing his fingers around the opening. He eased it open and peered inside. "Henry, take a look at this."

"My god."

Before them, dusted wooden steps descended into darkness. Red bricks lined the walls, caked in dew-glistening spider webs. Peter couldn't believe the sight. Somewhere down there, Jerry Fisher hid.

"Jesus Christ," Henry said, making Peter jump. "Sorry, kid . . . I'm just in shock he told the truth about this place. *Look* at this thing."

Peter couldn't articulate how he felt. The sight reminded him of something from an old school horror movie, something with Vincent Price and clueless victims.

Not unlike now . . .

Peter kept his voice low. "I want to get down there before I lose my courage. Follow me."

With a deep breath, he crawled inside the opening. Crouched on all fours, he guided himself with his hands, feeling where to go. The cold floor pressed into his palms, making his arms break out in gooseflesh. Then he felt the wood of the steps. Behind him, he heard Henry grunt as the old man struggled to stay behind.

"All good?" Peter whispered. "Slow and steady, just keep moving."

"All good. Don't worry."

Easier said than done, Peter thought. *You go head over ass and you're taking me with you, Henry . . .*

Peter never imagined himself to be claustrophobic until that moment. With Henry directly behind him, inky darkness pressed in from all sides. The walls seemed too close, the ceiling too low. Even if he'd wanted to, Peter couldn't open his arms to full length. He couldn't scoot backwards if needed, either. The only way was forward, one hand at a time. And if Fisher had set a trap . . .

Peter's hand connected with packed, cold earth. He decided not to tell Henry he'd reached the bottom and instead eased himself up as quiet as possible. He heard Henry take the last step and stand, too.

Where the hell are we?

Feeling around in the darkness, Peter's hand met the gnarled and hard wood of a door. He skimmed his fingers around, discovering a new texture, rough and solid.

A handle, He thought.

He could see the door in his mind's eye, the wood grayed and the handle rusted. Peter pressed against the door, slowly adding more weight. The door eased open without a sound. He felt around the inner wall, staying as silent as his body would permit. His heart rammed his chest like a kick drum and he worried the whole house could hear it. A hand patted his back, forcing a gasp. Peter turned, despite not being able to see, and Henry apologized.

"Got to be a light switch, hold on."

Peter felt something small and plastic protruding from the wall and sighed with relief before thumbing the switch down, filling the room with a piss-yellow glow. The cellar looked empty.

"I don't see him," Henry said, keeping his voice low.

On the left, ancient looking barrels flanked the moss covered stone walls in racks, their wooden lids damp and shining. An organic rot filled the air, musty and stale, but ghosting just beneath lay the sharp scent of fermenting wine. Another odor made Peter gag, putrid and rotten. The smell of spoiled meat. Two wooden tables stood to the right, the closest covered by an indecipherable misshapen heap. Peter squinted and waited for his eyes to adjust.

"Oh . . . Jesus . . ." he said. "I think it's Shelly."

As Peter's vision cleared, the mass on the table came into focus. A long transparent tube tailed off to the floor where it coiled in rings like a headless snake. It reminded Peter of a novelty condom. Thin blue veins lined its length, and when his brain finally registered the sight, Peter fought back the urge to throw up.

That's Shelly's large intestine . . .

A slop of stretched flesh covered the top of the table, bone protruding from innards in a stew of gore. The blood had dried some time ago, now browned like unused paint. In the mess on the floor, white lumps of what looked like curdled milk or bacon fat hardened. "Jesus Christ," Henry whispered. "How could someone do this?"

They moved towards the table, the putrid smell growing stronger. Peter winced. "Look there. It's Jamie."

On the second table, Jamie Peters' body lay twisted and distorted. Better shape than Shelly Matthews, but not much.

"It's like they exploded," Henry said. "That sick, sick monster."

Peter held up Jamie's arm. Rigor mortis had come and gone, the limb returning to its loose state. Stretch marks lined the skin, and from the feel, Peter knew inside were shattered bones.

"He stretched Jamie out," Peter said, dropping the arm back to the table and wiping his hands on his jeans. "I don't mean to sound crude, but it's as Donald said, like trying to fit on a new jacket a size too small. And look at Shelly. She's *destroyed*. Neither of them were a good fit."

"Did you notice the stretches all over Walter? The marks were everywhere. Looked like Phobos just about managed to squeeze in there and keep calm."

Peter couldn't look away from Jamie's body. "Do you think he can use Walter again?"

"We can only hope not."

Something shuffled in the shadows.

Peter swung around and eyed the barrels on the far wall. The light flickered overhead with a zapping noise. Peter heard his own neck creak in the silence. Then someone spoke.

"Don't hurt me . . ."

"Jerry?"

A filthy hand appeared around the corner of an end barrel. Squinting in the light, Jerry Fisher stepped out into the room.

Peter guessed the man had been pressed behind the wine rack all along, flattened against the stone wall. The space looked so constricted that Peter thought there couldn't be enough room to take a full breath without feeling pressure.

"You're here to hurt me," Jerry said. "Aren't you?"

Fisher looked like a madman, his eyes vibrating in their sockets. Dust caked his black polo neck, his skin dirty and blotched. His hair stood up at awkward clumps, as if he'd been tearing at it. Or if someone else had. His right cheek was swollen to the size of a tennis ball.

Well, Peter thought. *Paul told the truth about getting him in the face with the crowbar . . . He looks absolutely psychotic.*

Peter's throat clicked as he tried to swallow. Jerry's right hand was hidden behind his back. "What've you got there, Jerry?"

"I know why you're here." Jerry sounded sedated, his voice docile and dreamlike. "You've come to hurt me."

"No. *No.* We just want to talk . . . Show us what's behind your back."

Slowly, Jerry revealed the crowbar. "It's just this thing," He said. "That's all."

"Put it down."

Jerry eyed the bat like a lover, turning it over gently in his palms. "You've come to hurt me. That's what you're here to do. I know you."

Peter's voice broke. "Not true. Now put it down."

Jerry's face twisted in a snarl, his lips quivering. His knuckles whitened around the bar. "*I know you!*"

"No!"

Fisher swung. Peter threw his arms in front of his face, deflecting a whack of the crowbar. It bounced off his forearm, a bite of pain blooming instantly. Peter balked and reached for the weapon, his shaking hands clasping the metal as he wrested the bar free.

"*Drop it!*"

They smacked to the stone wall, both snarling like feral dogs. Peter's arms trembled from the hit, but he ignored the pain and whipped the crowbar first to the left, then the right, trying to loosen Jerry's grip.

"Drop it!"

Useless words, Peter knew, but they still came out of instinct.

"Jerry, drop the goddamn bar!"

"Uh!"

Jerry pulled to the right, sending them both staggering up the room, the crowbar keeping them glued as one. Henry reached for Jerry as they passed, wrapping his arms around the counselor's neck. Jerry's eyes bulged, trashing like a wild animal avoiding captivity.

Spit flew from his lips. "Let go of me!"

He threw his body in a frenzy, trying to toss Henry from his back, but the old man held tight. Peter grasped the crowbar and yanked, but the mad man wouldn't let go. Then they crashed into the table where Shelly Matthews lay.

Peter's lower back pressed into the squishy, cold meat of the carcass. He cried out as Jerry crammed him against the table, the counselor fighting to free himself of Henry. A smell wafted from the disturbed corpse, making Peter gag, then Shelly's body slopped from the table and splashed to the floor. Peter's back arched over the table, the hard wood forcing its way into the center of his spine. The weight of Jerry and Henry pressed him harder and harder. He couldn't breathe. Still, he held the crowbar, his lungs burning. With a grunt, he forced the weapon down to his right side. The crowbar shuddered from the opposing force.

Jerry cried out and tried to wrench the weapon back, his eyes bulging from their sockets and his face purpling as Henry squeezed. Spittle flew from his lips.

His voice came out a gargle. "Let it *go!*"

He yanked hard and the three men stumbled onto the destroyed corpse of Shelly Matthews. And slipped.

They shouted in unison, crashing to the mess of spoilt innards, shattered bone and rotting flesh. Cold liquid seeped through Peter's shirt and jeans, kissing his skin. Bile rose in the back of his throat that Peter fought to keep down.

Unfortunately, Jerry Fisher couldn't do the same.

The strangled man, his face now a deep shade of purple, vomited. It splashed from his lips, joining the rotting remains of the fermented body and missing Peter's face by inches. The counselor tried to swallow but Henry's arms locked tighter around his throat, keeping a mouthful of puke lodged.

He's going to choke to death!

Peter pulled the crowbar, his hands slick with sweat and gore and splashed in vomit.

One wrong move and this thing slips . . .

He whipped back and forth, his elbows working into the slop beneath him, fighting to find purchase. In his mind, Peter saw a kid's pool full of butcher waste and cringed. Then his left elbow slid from under him. The crowbar pulled free of Jerry's grasp.

Hands now free, Jerry reached for his throat, slapping to open Henry's grip.

"Stand up!" Henry ordered. "Get off him and stand up!"

Henry pulled Jerry by the throat and the two stumbled back, then Henry threw the counselor towards the far way. Jerry gasped for air, his complexion returning to normal. A slop of brown film from Shelly's corpse glistened on his clothes. He looked to Peter, his eyes full of hate.

Peter stumbled to his feet with the crowbar, his heart hammering. "You going to talk now?"

"You'll never get out of here alive," Jerry spat. His voice sounded like sandpaper, raw from acidic vomit and lack of air. "*None* of us are getting out alive. He won't allow it."

Peter's grip tightened on the crowbar. "You mean Phobos? We found your books, Jerry, we *saw* him. Now how in the world do we get rid of him?"

"You don't."

Peter and Henry exchanged a look of frustration, Henry breathing heavily through his nose.

"You called it here, you *have* to know how to send it back."

Fisher coughed and rubbed at his throat. "I would be killed. Harris Dawson's a very powerful man. He's the one with the money and the ideas. But even he's not to blame for this."

"What are you talking about?"

"Things happen in this world you wouldn't believe, Mr. Laughlin. I mean, would you honestly believe me if I told you this little, how should I call it? *Experiment?* Yes, experiment. That this little experiment of ours was funded by an external company? A legitimate tax-paying company?"

Henry shook his head and planted his hands on his hips. "What are you talking about, Fisher?"

"*They* know exactly what they're paying for when they funded Dawson. The big heads at the top of that company just don't want to get their hands dirty, that's all. So, instead, they seek out people such as Harris Dawson . . . People with an esoteric interest. Offer to fund their ventures."

"Why would they do that?"

"Control, Peter? Why else? Imagine the pure power one would possess if they managed to tame a *god*? Do I need to spell it out for you?"

"And where do you fit into all of this? What are you?"

"A hired hand. A contractor. Just a lower rung on the ladder. Dawson's research is funded by these people, he's contracted by them, and I'm contracted by Harris."

"If Harris is the one with the ideas, and he's the one they're funding, then why did he hire you?"

"We're old friends, Laughlin, and that's what friends do. Harris and I participated in linguistics courses back in college, something I was always better at. He asked me to decipher a family heirloom. A page. No prize money for guessing what I discovered. It took *months*, but together, we put enough of the pieces in place to have a clearer picture of what we possessed. I had no money, no job, no plan . . . And I loved to act." He smiled a toothy grin. "One afternoon, when Harris came to see me at the actors' society rendition of Hamlet, his eyes absolutely beamed. He had a plan. He always did. He could earn us a living. Some people had been to see him, he said. Men in Black, he called them, only half joking. They knew what his family possessed, that page, and it interested them greatly. They offered to fund a project for Dawson, one to continue his research on other papers. Can you believe, I was simply trying to make a go in the entertainment industry up until that point. I wanted to be an actor."

"Fisher," Peter said, gritting his teeth. "How do we destroy this thing? Tell us."

Jerry massaged his throat. "I'm telling you what I know, Peter. Context is important . . . You see, Dawson knows things about this universe that if others heard, they would disregard as the ravings of a lunatic. He'd be locked up. But with funding from *The People*, as Harris called them, we were free to explore our new discovery. They had even more pages for us . . . And when we figured out what was written on those pages . . . My god."

"This is insane," Henry said. He rubbed at his temples. "Absolutely crazy."

"There are books in this world that would melt your brain to read, Mr. Randolph," Jerry said. "*De Vermis Mysteriis* for example, or even the discovered writings of Frank Carpenter, although they are considered drivel by many. There's *The Necronomicon* . . . Many, many more. And each hold a grain of the real truth."

Peter shook his head. "The Necronomicon? That's fiction, right?"

Jerry chuckled. "Wrong. Very wrong. There are monsters, gods I would call them, desperate to get back into this world, Peter. And they'll stop at nothing to do so. I believe you've met one already."

"Phobos . . ." Henry said the name like an unwanted chunk of phlegm caught in his throat. "And those books upstairs, are they copies of this Necro-something?"

"Oh my, no. They are nothing more than feeble transcripts and hand-me-down tales, told by men who only *wished* to gaze their eyes upon the one true sacred book. Chinese whispers, if you will. Even the *Necronomicon* pales in comparison to the *true* book. But, each holds a grain derived from the original. Some sliver of importance, but never the whole thing. One should not take a single teaching as the entire truth. That's where the world's belief denominations are off the mark. The works of John Dee, *The Golden Chain of Homer*, the writings of Aleister Crowley, Frazer's *The Golden Bough*, *Dogme et Rituel de la Haute Magie*, the *Theatrum Chemicum*, hell, even the Judeo-Christian Bible, all contain *some* piece of the greater puzzle."

Henry rubbed his eyes. "If you and this *company* only have pages, who owns the *real* book?"

"The real book?" With that, Jerry clapped his hands and barked a laugh. "Mr. Randolph, *no one has the* whole *book!* The pages are scattered far and wide. If one man held the entire thing, he'd hold all the power of the universe! All Harris and I have are these Chinese-whisper books and hand-me-down tales. A little piece of truth sprinkled here and there, that's all . . . But those tiny sprinklings can be very helpful. They're clues. What I do, Mr. Randolph, is look for similarities within the texts and the writings of our pages, and try to find a lead."

"Why do you do this?"

Fisher's face fell. "To call something more powerful than you could ever imagine into this world. For it to be grateful, and in return, bestow more power than you could ever dream of on both myself and Harris Dawson. We would be the rulers of this world, don't you see? And all others, every last one of you, would bow before us . . . And just so you know, we would have prayed to *any* of the gods we discovered. *Any* of them. It just so happens that the pages we got our hands on told the tale of Phobos. *The Great God of Fear.*"

A wave of dizziness overcame Peter and he gripped the wall for support. He looked to Fisher. "You mean there are more of these things?"

With a shake of the head, Fisher said, "Many, many more . . . And now Phobos now exists on our plane of existence. *He's here.* Once He finds a suitable host and is strong enough to grow within it, the transition between the Otherworld and ours will be complete. He will be here to stay."

"And you honestly believe that he won't waste you as easily as he'd waste the rest of us? You *honestly* believe this company funding Dawson's research won't just dispose of you once they know your work is done now that Phobos is here?"

Jerry looked confused. "People believe in stranger things all the time, Peter. Suicide bombers blow themselves to smithereens in the name of their creator. People go to war all over the world because they believe their god said so, or because their country did, and what is country worship without liking it to godly? The only difference is I can *see* my god with my own two eyes. That tends to persuade me . . . And He's here all because of me." Fisher looked to Henry, then to Peter. "You can kill me now, if you wish. It doesn't make a difference in the long run. My job's finished. Whether I rule here alongside Phobos and Harris, or you kill me and my Lord sends me to the Otherworld, it's all the same."

"No," Peter said. "No, that would be too easy. You've got more answers. Like how to stop him." He gave Fisher a steady stare. "There's something in one of those books, isn't there? I couldn't quite place it at first, but now it's making sense. Why the books were littered on the floor. You *have* thought about Dawson and that company killing you, haven't you? You were getting a backup plan. Insurance. Figuring out a way to stop Phobos in case they betrayed you."

Something flashed in Jerry's eyes.

"Deep down, you're scared of it, too . . . What can stop it, Jerry?"

Jerry backed towards the cellar door. "I bow before my god, and take no false gods before Him."

Peter stalked forward, crowbar in hand. "You're a liar. You marked those pages in those books because there's something there. What is it, huh? A ritual? What makes him disappear?"

Jerry didn't answer. Peter lifted the crowbar.

"You're going to send him back where he came from."

CHAPTER FIFTEEN

Banging came from the staircase outside the cellar door.

"Is this your backup?" Jerry asked. "The cavalry coming to do away with me?"

Peter flexed his jaw. "We're not going to hurt you, because you're going to stop this creature once and for all. Or else you're going to tell us how to."

"Fine, fine."

The door burst open and Donald fell inside, his pants dirty from the crawl downstairs. Spotting Jerry Fisher, his eyes turned to slits. "You, you fuck." He jabbed a finger at the man. "You're a dead man."

Peter's heart raced. "Donald, wait—"

Donald took the room in two strides and swung at Jerry's face. The punch connected with a dull thump and Jerry hit the floor. Donald straddled him, his weight pressing down on the man's chest. "You're a fuckin' dead man, Fisher!"

He brought his fists down again and again, Jerry's head flopping from side to side with sharp smacks. Peter dropped the crowbar and rushed to Donald, pulling at the man's shoulders. Donald swatted him away and continued his beating. The large man managed to get five more hits in before Henry was at him, too, ripping at Donald's sweater.

Henry sounded frantic. "Donny! Stop it, please!"

Donald wouldn't listen. His fists fell like anvils, mashing Jerry's face to a pulp. Peter's stomach churned as a puddle of dark red pooled around the man's head, carrying two knocked out teeth.

"Jesus, Don, you'll kill him! Stop!"

Donald roared, full of pent-up rage. Spittle flew from his lips and his hair fell into his face. Peter knew the adrenaline and primal rage coursing through his veins had taken over. Donald was seeing red.

"Peter," Henry said. "The crowbar!"

Peter rushed and scooped it from the ground, steadying it like a baseball bat and eyeing the back of Donald's head.

No, he thought. *Not there, could cause serious damage . . . I only want him to stop, I don't want to hurt him . . . Or give Phobos another body to host . . . His back. Yes. His back.*

But what if Donald's high adrenaline rendered the hit useless and he turned on him and Henry? Could they take him down, even with two on one and a crowbar? Either way, Peter had to do *something*, because Donald's hands came down again and again, getting slower. Each hit now sounded like he punched a bag of overripe tomatoes. His right fist came up, smothered in red, shaking, and he paused.

"That's enough," Peter said, his voice weak. "That's enough, Donny. Stand up, now . . . You've done enough."

Donald pushed himself off the man. He wiped his face, smearing it with blood. Tears glistened in his red, swollen eyes and his shirt clung to him, almost transparent with sweat. His shoulders jerked as he blubbered.

"Sick fuck had to die. He had to, right?" Donald looked between Peter and Henry. "I was right to do it, weren't I?"

Peter lowered the crowbar behind his back, hoping Donald wouldn't take any notice. He kept his voice calm. "Let's get back upstairs, what do you say? Come on. Paul's waiting. There's nothing left for us down here now."

"Paul's fuckin' dead."

Oh, Donald, Peter thought. *What have you done?*

Henry took a step forward, making Peter wince. *Don't get close, Henry!*

Henry cocked his head to the side. "Did you kill him?"

A look of genuine shock passed over Donald's face. "Me? Christ, no. Started hemorrhaging on the couch right after you guys left. I think *this* bastard musta given him a brain aneurism when he hit him on the head with that bar."

Donald's eyes went to the crowbar.

"You can drop it, kid. I ain't gonna hurt neither of you. You know I had to do what I done."

Peter released the crowbar and it clattered to the ground

behind him. "We needed him, Donny. He had answers. He knew how to stop this thing."

"You're dumber than ya look if you think he would've told us jack shit."

"Oh yeah? Well then we would have *made* him tell us. You know Phobos might be able to use Jerry's body now. Even if you ruined his head."

Donald tried maintaining a blank expression but his eyes gave him away. For a brief instant, Peter saw that Donald knew he'd let his anger take control. Maybe even given Phobos another chance to host. Still, Peter knew Donald's stubbornness would hold out. He didn't take him as a man to apologize.

Donald arched an eyebrow and nodded towards the door. If he noticed Shelly Matthews' burst-open body on the floor, or Jamie Peters' remains on the nearby table, he didn't say a word. He noticed something else, though.

"Look at that. Laundry shoot. Same as the one in the lady's room. Guess that solves one mystery. Must've ran to it and screamed up for help. Sound travelled . . . And there's us thinkin' she was in her room." He shook his head. "We gonna go back upstairs now?"

"Sure," Peter said. His body ached and he needed to sleep. Too much had happened. "Lead the way."

As Donald started up the stairs, Peter looked to Jerry Fisher's body on the floor, his stomach roiling.

Definitely dead . . . No doubt about that. Jesus . . .

Using his bare hands, Donald had shattered the man's skull. Jerry's nose hung from a thread on his right cheek as blood pooled and glistened, collecting in the facial cavity. Peter shook his head in bewilderment and turned for the stairs. Their only hope of escaping died with Fisher, who now meant nothing more than a dinner bell to flies and maggots . . . *Or*, Peter thought, *to something far worse . . . Why didn't Donald think of that?*

Henry closed the cellar door behind them, cutting the light and plunging the staircase into darkness. None of them said a word as they climbed up into the kitchen and made for the living room. Once there, Peter looked to the couch where Paul had been.

"Where is he?"

"He was here," Donald said, raising an open hand. "I swear. Started shakin' and shit when you guys went down to the cellar. I tried callin' you but you mustn't have heard me. Tried pinnin' him down but he just kept convulsin'. I'm tellin' ya, that blow Jerry gave him knocked his brains loose." Donald's eyes widened. "You think that creature got him like it got Walter?"

Peter stifled the anger building inside him. Donald should've stayed with Paul and let him and Henry deal with Fisher. Like the plan had been. But, of course, Peter knew Donald shot first and questioned later. With a sigh, Peter informed Donald what Fisher had told them.

". . . But even Harris isn't the leader in all this. If that company hadn't given him the funds, maybe Harris would've let the whole thing lie and never pursued."

"But they *did* fund the fuck, and he *did* pursue," Donald said.

"And Phobos is here now," Henry said. "Fisher paid for it with his own life."

"You think this company will show up? Come in blazin' with a SWAT team or some shit? You think they know this Phobos thing is here?"

"We won't give them the chance," Peter said. "We're not letting this creature loose on the world. We're stopping it once and for all. Tonight."

Donald laughed with no humor. "Three strung-out fucks are gonna stop an ancient evil god?"

"That's exactly what we're going to do."

Henry rubbed at his forehead. "Speaking of addiction, I swear I'd do anything for a drink right now. Bourbon on the rocks. That's pretty funny, right? The world I know gets turned on its ass and my brain bounces back to alcohol."

"The hook sure is deep," Peter said. "Every time we even have the smallest break, I'm thinking of a drink, too. Or a smoke. It's insane. But fuck me, what I'd do for a beer right now."

"Well," Donald said. "Let's just take it one step at a time, all right? Look, Phobos took Paul's body and it's in pretty good shape besides the beatin' he took off Fisher. He's around here somewh—"

As if in response, Paul stumbled into the room. Peter jumped and pulled the other two men back, his heart racing and his skin crawling. The deadman stood in the doorway, his damaged head lowered, saliva dripping to the floor.

Henry covered his mouth. "Jesus Christ . . . Look at him!"

Paul's body was contorted out of proportion, as if Phobos wore his flesh like clothing two sizes too small. His right elbow jutted through the skin, the bone covered in ribbons of torn muscle. His stomach, which had been flat and in good shape when Paul lived, now spilled over his jeans as if pumped full of fat. His knees bent from the weight, Paul shuffling inside, dragging his feet along the ground. He raised his head.

"Howdy, boys."

The deadman's head jutted at odd angles, stretched by the daemon. His broken skull pushed at his bald head like a balloon full of rocks. One eye sat an inch lower than the other, his crooked mouth leaking.

"Jesus Christ," Henry whispered.

"No Jesus here, Henry Randolph," Phobos said using Paul's mouth. His voice was mush, like dead leaves clogged in a pipe. "Jus' me."

Shuffling forward, Phobos reached out like a monster from one of those *Living Dead* movies. Then he moaned, pushing aside the broken door with his foot.

Donald whined. "What do we fuckin' do?"

The three men backed up, matching Phobos pace for pace. Paul's dead eyes fell about the three of them, slithering from one to the other. Peter had a moment to wonder if the creature used the eyes like the organs were intended or if he saw through some other means. Looking into them, Peter saw no life, only two glossy balls falling about inside their sockets.

Peter's stomach tightened. After all they'd been through, after all they'd heard and seen, now he feared Phobos. He couldn't deny it.

Peter's back hit the wall, and Phobos leaped. They crashed to the floor.

Fuck!

The weight bore down, making it hard to breathe. The fatty stomach rolled about, squishing Peter's ribs like a waterbed filled of raw meat. Peter grimaced and batted at the creature's shoulders, his breath unable to reach his lungs.

The deadman's face crawled inches from Peter's, the lifeless eyes unfocused. A trail of spit dripped from those blue lips, tapping to Peter's cheek, icy and wet. Phobos gnashed Paul's teeth together, cracking one in the process.

Peter wheezed. *"Help . . . "*

Over Paul's disfigured head, he saw the other two trying. They pulled at the bloated arms, ripping them back with yells of frustration. If either let go, Phobos' face would crash into Peter's, sinking those cracked teeth into his cheek.

Oh god, Peter thought. *Please don't lose your grip, please, please, please!*

Peter saw it in his mind's eye—Phobos' teeth clicking together just as Donald or Henry lost their grip, sending those cold, snapping teeth into the flesh of his cheek. The creature would chomp down, emitting an explosion of excruciating pain. Peter would scream as warm blood saturated his face. Then Phobos would tear a ribbon of skin away and shake it like a hungry dog.

"Get him off of me!"

Stars swam before his eyes in a black sea, winning over his field of vision. Peter cried out, his lungs burning, his voice far away to his own ears.

I'm going to die, I'm not going to catch another breath . . .

Peter's fingers grew cold and tingled. An involuntary moan escaped his lips.

Phobos' face fell another inch and warmth radiated from the deadman's skin. Paul's body hadn't even gone cold yet.

Peter's ears filled with the sound of his own throbbing blood. His eyes pulsed in time. Someone moved about the room, but Peter's mind drifted. He couldn't concentrate. Not even when the cold enamel of Paul's teeth pressed his cheek, and slowly began to close . . .

Air rushed to his lungs like a vacuum. Peter's arms closed over his chest where the creature no longer sat. He bolted up, his legs thrumming in agony. Shaking, he fell for the couch, unaware of his surroundings. Slowly, the room returned to normal.

"Peter, can you breathe?"

Henry, Peter thought. *It's Henry.*

He tried to breathe but only managed a wheeze.

Donald tackled the fuck, Peter thought, his mind slowly returning to normal. *He let go and charged the bastard . . .*

Donald pinned Phobos to the floor, just as he had Jerry Fisher. A string of obscenities flew from the man's mouth as he brought his bloody fists down again and again.

He's going to cave his head in, Peter thought. *So Phobos will flee and have to find another host!*

"Henry, come on."

They ran to Donald who lay in another barrage of flying fists.

"I'll kill you!" Donald roared. His vocal chords sounded in danger of tearing from the force. "*Yasonofabitch, I'll fuckin' kill you!*"

It happened so fast that both Peter and Henry skidded to a halt. Like a snake striking its prey, Phobos whipped Paul's head up and bore those broken and bloody teeth. He struck for Donald's throat—and bit.

Donald screamed, throwing one final fist into the creature's deformed face. Paul's head cracked the floorboards. Donald staggered, blood spilling down his shirt, and fell against the wall. A gurgle escaped his mouth, his face losing color. Eyes shining with terror, he looked to Peter and removed his hands from his throat, letting out a gush of crimson.

Peter shook his head, his legs weak. His mouth moved, but no words came.

Donald fell.

He crashed face down onto the floor with a sickening thump, blood pooling beneath him. He twitched once, then lay still.

"No . . . No, no, no . . ."

Beside Donald, the deformed deadman rose, his jaw working on the chunk of Donald's throat. His voice came garbled. "*Nothing like Italian meat to placate hunger . . .*"

Rage boiled inside Peter, coursing through his veins and forcing his hands into tight fists. An image of Beth with their newborn child flashed in his mind. How could he have let his guard down and allowed this creature to frighten him? He *had* to get home.

Without thinking, Peter charged Phobos. He wrenched his foot back and kicked the deadman square in the nose. A revolting crack rang out as Paul's head flew back, then the body hit the ground.

Peter brought his foot down again and again on the deadman's face, continuing the job where Donald had stopped. If Phobos wanted to try and strike him now, he'd have a hard time doing so- Peter mashed the lower jaw to a pulp. Bone resisted beneath his heel before giving way with a stomach-turning crack. Each lift of his foot revealed a more disgusting sight.

Paul's body no longer moved. His lifeless eyes had closed. Phobos had left.

"Donald," Henry said. "Jesus Christ, he's dead, Peter."

Peter looked to the man on the floor. A wave of sorrow washed over him. Donald had been hotheaded, true, but he'd only been looking out for the three of them in the long run. After all, how was he to know that Jerry Fisher had any answers, or was willing to give them up? Donald only saw *the enemy*. And he tried to put a stop to said enemy the only way he knew how— with brute force. For Peter and for Henry, he had tried.

So much blood . . .

"Peter, is he gone? That bastard, is he gone?"

"In search of another host."

Henry's eyes widened. He wiped tears from his eyes. "Then we have to . . . You know what."

"What?"

Henry sniffled. "We need to damage Donald's body. That fucking bastard can possess him. Use the body, right?"

"No, Henry—"

"You know as well as I do that we need to do this." Henry coughed, tears rolling down his cheeks. "It's the *right thing!*"

"But maybe Phobos can't, maybe, I mean—"

"Peter!" Henry's eyes vibrated in their sockets. "He used everyone who's died so far except for Fisher, now I'm thinking it's because of the state of the body, what's the use? We need to do this or this thing can host again."

Peter sighed. "How do we do it?"

"It removed itself from Paul when you destroyed the head." Henry took a moment to collect himself, looking to the roof and blinking away fresh tears. "Maybe it could still possess the body, but in the long run I'm guessing it would be no use. With Walter, all those cuts and the sliced open stomach, I'm guessing that's not much use anymore, either. Phobos needs a body in a good a condition as he can get it. So he can shape it in the form of himself. His *real* shape. Didn't you see that with Paul? He was completely deformed."

"Still doesn't answer how we should do it."

Henry sighed. He pinched the bridge of his nose and squeezed. "Fuck it," he said. "I'll do it. We just need to get it done, that's all that matters. And ruining the damn head like you guys just did seems to work . . . Phobos must have trouble if the brain is damaged." He lifted himself from the floor. "Let's make it as difficult as we can for him."

Peter stayed silent. Henry sniffled.

"I'm so sorry, Donny. I'm so very, very sorry."

Henry stood above the man and took a deep breath. Peter guessed if he had a moment to doubt himself, he'd freeze.

No overthinking . . . Thank you for being the one to do it, Henry . . .

Squeezing his eyes shut, Peter clasped his hands over his ears. He felt the ground thump with every stomp of Henry's boot, ringing up his legs and through his body. He heard Henry grunt, the sound muffled, with each hit. Then came a crack, followed by a dreadful squelch. Then, nothing.

"Peter, help me with the carpet. Please."

Peter opened his eyes. Henry stood before him, panting and covered in sweat. Gore caked the bottom of the old man's jeans. Instead of looking there, Peter looked Henry in the eye and nodded. They dragged the carpet from the center of the room, covering the unspeakable ruins of Donald's remains. Peter looked to the ceiling and tried shake free the glimpse he caught of Donald's crushed head. He blinked away tears that threatened to overspill.

"Hey," Henry said, giving his shoulder a squeeze. "It's done."

Peter stepped away, the sight of Donald's form wrapped in the white carpet making him ill. It reminded him of some fat, unnatural worm.

"The curtains," Henry panted. "To cover Paul, too."

Together, they tore the curtains from the window frame and covered Paul's remains, hiding the despicable sight.

Henry planted his hands on his hips and sniffled. "It's a nightmare . . . We're the only ones left."

"But he can't get us now. We just have to wait for the snow to thaw. Then we make a run for it. If he could leave this place, he would have already . . ."

"He ruptured Jamie Peters' body to pieces, you don't think that's still usable, do you?"

Peter shook his head. "No. He tried already. We're all that's left. All he can do is conjure up something from our subconscious, try and project our fears and make us take our own lives. But we're not going to let that happen. We'll figure out a way to destroy this thing, once and for all."

Fear licked across Peter's stomach as a new idea hit. He hated himself for not having the notion sooner.

Oh, please, let me be wrong . . .

"He's gotten a lot of practice squeezing into fresh bodies," Peter said, his mouth dry. "Henry . . . This might sound crazy, but . . . Where's the cat?"

CHAPTER SIXTEEN

A noise bellowed from the hallway, making Peter's skin crawl and his hair stand on end.

He remembered hearing two tom cats fight outside his window once when he was a teenager. He'd shot out of bed like it was on fire. At first, it sounded like a distressed baby. His heart entered the back of his throat while he made his way to the window and peeked out the curtains. But of course, there'd been no abandoned baby. Instead, two stray alley cats hissed and circled one other, their hair and haunches raised. Peter watched until one made that noise again, just like a baby wailing.

The noise from the hallway sounded the very same. Only amplified, and guttural.

The size, Peter thought. *Oh Christ, the thing must be gigantic . . .*

"Henry," He said, his legs wanting to give out. "Alisa . . . The damn cat . . ."

Henry whispered, his eyes wide. "I know, keep quiet . . ."

The creature purred from the hallway.

"He's toying with us," Peter said. "Same as any cat . . . Henry, what? What is it?"

Scrunching his face, Henry said, "Something's on the tip of my tongue . . . An idea . . . Just can't make it out yet. Slips my mind every time. Give me a second."

"I don't know if we have a second, Henry."

Henry raised a finger to shush him. Outside, the creature slowly paced, its claws clicking the floorboards. Peter watched the hollow doorframe, his heart racing, expecting it to enter at any moment. Then the creature slunk by, not looking in, and was gone. Peter's heart bashed his ribcage.

Like a mutated panther, He thought. *Oh Jesus . . .*

The cat's black hulk blended with the darkness like a moving shadow, only those glistening eyes gave it away as a separate entity. Passing the doorway a second time, it shot another glance.

It's trying to scare us to death . . . And it's working.

"I don't think it's going to stay out there for much longer, Henry. We need to do something quick."

"Oh my god . . ."

"What? *What is it?*"

Henry jogged to the fireplace, scooping up the leather bound book he'd been skimming through earlier that day. His fingers frantically worked the pages until he something. He held the book up to Peter.

"The illustration again?" Peter's patience ended. "What about it?"

"Peter, it's the *sea*. *Mare*, see, written there?" Henry tapped the page. "Like the French word. It must be the same in *this* language. The sea, Peter!"

"I don't know what you're talking about!"

Henry spoke fast. "Fisher said each one of these texts contained some grain of truth. He mentioned the Bible. I know that the King James version mentions *salt* over thirty times as a repellant to evil spirits. Pagans, Wiccans, all of the occult, use it as a cleansing aid for bad or evil energies. I couldn't place it at first, but Jerry must have known because—"

"There was no salt at breakfast?"

"Not *just* that, think, Peter."

The idea hit so hard that Peter's legs nearly buckled. "Walter's ice cream ingredients. Rock salt."

"Correct."

Peter studied the illustration, a vast ocean, the waves depicted by black curving lines. A sun set on the horizon, the sky caked in thick clouds. The title above read: *Mare, quae esta vitae fonnes.*

"Are you sure?" Peter asked. "Are you sure it will work? You think that thing can't stand salt?"

"I only know what you know. But from this chapter, even though I can't understand the text, the illustration and Jerry's reaction to the rock salt is the nearest thing to an answer that I can come up with. He *knew* it could repel Phobos, he knew it!"

"Oh, Jesus." Peter rubbed at his forehead. "There's salt circling the fucking yard! A *precaution*! He's stuck here!"

"Until Dawson comes and breaks the seal," Henry said. "In return for a favor, I'm guessing. Check and mate. We won't give him the chance to leave."

"Where is it? The canister of salt?"

"I have no idea."

"I saw it in a grocery bag, back when Andrew picked it up, but someone moved it. Most likely to the kitchen. Come on."

"That thing is out there."

"What other choice do we have, Henry? We have to make a break for it. You think you can do that?"

"I'll have to, won't I?"

Peter nodded. "Wait."

At fire place, Peter scooped the final two broken legs of the table. Splinters covered their business ends, perfect for stabbing.

If it comes to that . . . Fuck, I wish I still had that damned crowbar . . . Or . . .

Peter cursed. "There's a damn *shotgun* in the hallway, Henry! The gun rack!"

"We don't have a key. And if we spent more than two second out there fiddling with a lock or trying to smash the thing open, that cat would be on us quicker than you could say *shit*. You know that."

"I'll get it, somehow. Soon as I have the opportunity." He took a deep breath. "Let's go."

Racing from the living room, a single word whirled around Peter's mind:

Fuck, fuck, fuck, fuck, fuck, fuck . . .

His skin prickled as they entered the hallway, and from the staircase, the creature mewled.

"Come, on!"

Peter elbowed open the dining-room door and slammed it shut behind them. A second later, the cat crashed against the door, its weight shaking Peter's hands.

"*Fuck*! The breakfast table, Henry! Pull it here!"

The cat roared. Henry grabbed the sturdy piece of wood and dragged it across the floor, jarring it against the door just as a second crash hit. The table jittered, but Peter forced his weight against it, keeping it in place.

"It's not going to hold, we need something else."

Henry eyes darted frantically around the room.

Everything but the kitchen sink, Peter thought, unable to resist the joke. *Good Christ I need a drink.*

The thick wooden armchairs caught Peter's attention. He ordered Henry to grab one and the old man slid it over, packing it against the far side of the table. They hoisted the other two on top, adding weight. Peter held an armchair while Henry continued throwing objects onto the barricade—an old fashioned television set, the television cabinet, a couch he slid from the far end of the room. The creature hissed from the other side of the door and smashing its mass into the frame, but the barricade filled the space between an outcrop of wall and the door, lodging it in place.

"Oh thank Christ," Henry said, wiping at his face. "Think it'll hold?"

"Not for long. Do you see it anywhere? The salt?"

The creature hissed and cracked the door. A small split appeared in the wood.

Henry cocked a thumb over his shoulder. "The kitchen. Hurry."

They pushed open the swing door, entering the small cooking quarters. Peter went straight to the cabinets above the ovens and sink, pulling them open and rummaging through the contents. His hands shook.

Just one fucking drink would sort that out, he told himself. *You've had these shakes a million times before, remember? Nothing a quick shot or smoke wouldn't fix.*

"I don't see it," Henry called, his voice filled with panic. "The back door, Peter, the back door, we could try and make a break for it."

An image of the two scrambling through the dense snowfall came to Peter. The thick black feline would pounce through the powder, gaining with ease. They'd be lucky to make it halfway across the yard.

"Useless, Henry. Come on, now, I need you to stay focused.

We need to find—"

Behind a half-used bag of floor and a can of coffee, the white and blue bag sat unopened.

"I found it!" Peter pulled the bag free, his hands shaking. "How do we—"

The dining room door cracked, echoing throughout the room like a gunshot. From the other side of the kitchen door, Phobos roared, the mutated sound making Peter's stomach roil. One of the leather arm chairs tumbled from the barricade, then came the clatter of claws.

Peter's fingers fumbled with the plastic wrapping as he let out a frustrated yelp.

"Hand me a knife, please! Quick!"

Henry pulled open the nearest drawer, whipping out a butcher knife.

"Here."

Peter worked the knife into the plastic, spilling salt to the floor. "Shit."

The granules looked thick and chunky.

Enough to damage the sonofabitch.

Claws bounded across the dining room. Peter wanted to vomit. Bracing himself, he clutched the bag in both hands and looked to Henry. "Get behind me."

The swing door crashed open as the giant cat fell inside the room, skidding on the tiles. Sores and broken bone jutted from wet and filthy fur. Roaring, it regained its balance and darted straight for the two men.

Without aim, Peter flung the contents of the bag.

The cat's head rammed his stomach, smashing him against the back door and crushing Henry beneath him. The wind flew from Peter's lungs, winding him. He grimaced and squeezed his eyes shut. Warm blood trickled down his leg, but Peter concentrated on something else- the fact the cat wasn't ripping his guts out. The rotten odor of singed hair and rotting flesh attacked his nose.

Peter opened his eyes and watched as the cat screeched and stumbled about the room. It knocked over pots and pans, jittering as if in the throes of a brain aneurism.

"There you go, you fucker!" Peter yelled. "Have a taste of your own medicine!"

The cat trashed about the room, tendrils of gray smoke trailing away from where the salt had connected. Peter's eyes widened when he saw just where he'd hit. Directly in the bastard's face.

Peter sucked a deep breath, his lungs trying to refuse. He knew he had to relax, for his muscles to let up and his body to return to normal, but under the circumstances, relaxing felt out of the question. He tried pushing himself off the floor but his legs betrayed him, sending his ass back to the ground. He whipped his head from side to side, flinging the sweat that trailed down his face. He watched Henry scurry against the cupboards, avoiding the creature's sharp nails as it blindly trashed.

The old man screamed in terror, the sound lost in Phobos' earsplitting roar. The alley cats Peter heard as a teenager paled beyond belief to what he heard now. If one sounded like this, the whole neighborhood would have shit themselves.

Phobos' tail whipped about, its head trashing from side to side. Then the mutated face began to bubble. Peter couldn't help compare the sight to tarmac on a hot day. The cat's eyes melted away like plastic, slopping down its furry face. Fangs as thick as Peter's middle finger hung from the creature's open mouth, the lips slithering away to nothing.

Gripping the rock salt, Peter considered lobbing another load, but to do so he'd have to stand and get halfway across the room. And right now, moving didn't seem possible. Warm blood soaked his leg, and Peter only now realized the damage Phobos had caused by barging into him. The monster had slashed his thigh, deep. Peter sucked air through his teeth and blinked away the hot tears filling his eyes. The skin was split from knee to foot. Blood saturated his jeans.

Henry's insistent calling finally cut through Phobos' wailing. "Peter! *Help me!*"

The large cat bellowed and slashed out in the direction of the old man's voice. If Henry hadn't moved his head just then, it would no longer be connected to his neck. But instead, the creature took a chunk from cupboard door. The wood spun across the floor, coming to rest at Peter's boot.

"Henry," he called. "Get into the stairwell, under the sink! Hide!"

Henry nodded and scrambled for the cupboard door. The cat seemed in too much pain to notice.

Good, Peter thought. *We've got the upper hand. For now.*

Henry threw open the cupboard door scrambled inside. He pulled it shut behind him, his frightened face visible through the now missing corner.

Phobos regained itself with a brisk shake of the head. A head that made Peter want to scream. Muscles flexed beneath stretched skin. Mewling, Phobos worked its razor-like claws into the floorboards, sinking them to the paw.

Stand, Peter. Get up . . .

Peter pushed himself from the floor with a gasp, his legs quivering as if he'd been electrocuted from the waist down. He cried out, working his back up the door, turning his face up as he went. His pulse beat in his neck, the bones in his legs aching. A hissing sound caught his attention, and Peter frowned.

The salt!

Grains spilled to the ground like an upturned egg timer. Peter balked and righted the bag. How much had he lost? Half? Maybe more?

Phobos' mutated nose quivered as it sniffed the air, seeking Henry.

Peter lurched across the floor, his feet straining to uphold him. Hot liquid dripped from his leg. He managed to get three steps before the pain became too much. Steadying himself, he called out. "Hey, you ugly bastard, you want some more?"

A purr rose from the creature's throat as the melted face swung in Peter's direction. Eyes, like burned plastic, had hardened to a black tar-like substance. Its tail worked back and forth, back and forth.

"Yeah, that's right. You want some more, you fuck?"

Phobos took a step towards the sound of Peter's voice.

Good boy, he thought. *That's it. Come to me.*

Phobos paused in the center of the kitchen, positioned between Peter and Henry. Behind its bulky frame, Peter watched

Henry's drained face stare back from the hole in the cupboard. He looked to be mouthing something, his lips trembling.

Phobos sank its nails further the floorboards, gaining purchase. Blind or not, Peter knew the cat would leap at any moment. Beside its paws lay ten dents the size of bullet holes, left by its butcher knife nails.

Peter put a shaking finger to his lips and stared Henry in the eye. *Quiet*, he tried to say. The old man nodded frantically, indicating he understood.

If you understand, then stop breathing so loud, Henry. Please. I can hear you from here . . .

Phobos kept its mutilated face pointed in Peter's direction, its nostrils flaring as it sniffed the air. A low, mewling noise came from deep within its throat like an engine idling.

It's gonna pounce . . .

When it did, Peter only hoped he'd be quick enough to react. He licked at his lips. They'd gone dry as ash. "Come on, baby . . . You wanna go, I'll go . . ."

Phobos slinked down, its haunches set. Thick muscles worked beneath the skin, rippling the tight flesh. The engine-like purr grew louder.

Peter clasped a handful of salt and braced himself. "Let's do it. Make your move."

Phobos didn't pounce. Instead, its back leg kicked out—right into Henry's face. Peter's eyes strained from their sockets.

"You fucking bastard! No!"

Phobos had been listening for Henry's breathing, all along. Peter rushed forward and chucked salt at the creature. Phobos screamed, making Peter wince. He thought his eardrums would blow. This time, the monster didn't smoke or sizzle.

This time it caught fire.

The disfigured body of Alisa fell towards the swing door, its fur a raging blaze. It missed the door, head-butting the wall, then fell through into the dining-room.

"Henry!"

Peter lurched towards the cupboard. A splash of blood dribbled down the white paint. Throwing open the ruined door, Peter gasped. Henry lay at the bottom of the staircase in a ragged heap.

"Henry? Can you hear me?"

Peter strained his ears as the old man moaned an unintelligible response. From the dining-room came a dull thump. The cat had collapsed.

"Henry, give me a second, okay?"

Rushing to the swing door, Peter peered into the living room, confirming his suspicion. Unlike in the movies when a supernatural entity died, the cat didn't dissipate into nothingness with a sizzle. Instead, it burned and burned, the smell of charred flesh and singed hair filling the space. Dark smoke packed the room. The fire alarm caught whiff and began screaming.

At least the fuck's without a body, Peter thought.

Getting on all fours, Peter crawled to the cellar with the bag of rock salt secured inside his jeans belt. The weight pressed his pelvis, reassuring him he could reach it if something happened. He pushed on a little more confident. The sharp smell of burned flesh and hair blossomed in the air and Peter breathed through his mouth to keep from gagging. Visible breath streamed from his lips as the house filled with smoke, his eyes stinging. He'd need to get Henry out before they suffocated. Above in the kitchen, the fire alarm continued to scream.

"Henry? Henry, get up."

The old man muttered and Peter hoisted him to his feet. With a gasp, Henry reached a shaking hand to his neck, clutching at the spot. Peter craned his neck to see better in the dim light and cursed. Blood glistened, coating Henry's neck and chest. Peter's stomach tightened.

"Jesus Christ, Henry, I didn't even have time to react, I'm so sorry."

"Hush up." Henry spoke from the corner of his mouth, his voice strained. "No time for that. Seeing colors here. I need to get something to stop the flow, it's bleeding badly, isn't it? I can't see it but I can feel it. It is, isn't it?"

"Here." Peter pulled off his shirt and handed it to Henry. Dark stains covered the garment from their struggle with Fisher, but it would have to do. Henry thanked him and took the shirt, removing his slick hand from the wound. Peter's eyes widened as he caught his first glimpse of the gash, a cut as sharp as a surgeon's incision, running from the right side of Henry's Adam's apple to just below his ear. Thin, but very deep. Beside the slice, Henry's jugular throbbed. Phobos had missed his target by mere inches.

"Missed the mark," Peter said, his voice breaking. "Aimed for an artery."

"Lucky me." Henry winced as he patted the wound with the shirt then held it out for inspected. A black, ink-like stain soaked through the cotton in the dim light. "Hell . . . I'm leaking something fierce, kid." Henry pressed the shirt back to his neck. "I need a hospital, or a medical professional. But somehow I just don't think that's going to happen." He sighed. "We need get out of here at the very least. Try think of some way of getting attention drawn to this place."

Back in the kitchen, the fire alarm continued screeching. Orange light danced to the wailing on the wall, coming from the dining room. Smoke hung low to the floor, curling around the room as it packed the place to capacity. Peter's lungs stung and he coughed, wiping at his eyes. He looked to Henry. "We blow this fucking place sky high." It was a statement, not a question. "How's that for attention?"

From the cellar door below, a muffled thump rang out. Then another.

Henry shot a glance to the kitchen cupboard. "What was that?"

"You know exactly what that is. Phobos is desperate. Come on, we need to get out, man. The smoke's getting too bad. Move."

The cellar door crashed open. Peter didn't look back. The dense black smoke forced him to squint. He grabbed a handful of Henry's shirt and broke for the dining room, pulling the old man behind. He held his breath as his pulse throbbed inside his neck and just behind his eyeballs.

As the kitchen door swung shut, thick clouds of toxic smoke puffed from around its frame. Peter darted through, the air agitating his eyes. He blinked fast, fighting his way to the hallway and dragging Henry behind. His shin bumped something hard.

A chair, Peter thought. *The goddamn barricade. We're going to choke to death in here!*

Closing his eyes, Peter kept one hand on Henry and felt about with the other. His palm connected with something solid and flat. The table. Clambering on top, Peter swung his legs down the other side and fell into the hallway. He sucked fresh air before turning to help Henry over, too. The old man's hand grabbed at thin air before clasping Peter's wrist. Peter pulled him through. Henry fell into the hallway, coughing and gagging as Peter wheezed down what little air he could.

He gagged, his throat tightening. "Henry, come on, outside."

Still clutching the filthy shirt to his neck, Henry nodded and followed.

Please make it, Peter thought. *After all this, please make it.*

The sight of the old man's waxy face made Peter want to cry out.

This isn't fair . . . Why Henry?

Peter sidestepped the shattered grandfather clock as the old man's hand clasped his shoulder. Ahead, the black rectangle of night and freedom beckoned.

"What is it?"

"Just wait . . ." Henry said.

Peter stopped just shy of the door as outside, something moved.

CHAPTER SEVENTEEN

"Someone's out there."

Snow crunched as something approached from out of sight. Peter's head reeled with confusion, his body telling him to run. With only himself and Henry left, and the town too far away for anyone to reach them, that left a body hosting Phobos. Peter stepped back, knocking into Henry.

"Whoever it is, they're coming fast. Move back."

A figure scrambled up porch on all fours, the boards of the steps groaning. Then it stood, and revealed a headless body.

"The living room, Henry! Go!"

The headless body of Jerry Fisher trashed about as it bolted for them, its snow covered hands grasping at thin air. It tripped on the shards of the clock and went sprawling to the floor. Glancing back as they reached the living room, Peter saw the body wasn't entirely headless. A smushed ball of pulp hung by threads to the neck, clumps of hair sprouting at odd angles and dried in blood.

"Stay here," Peter ordered. "You lose any more blood and you're going down. I'm taking care of this."

"You're bleeding, too, Peter! Don't be a fool!"

Ignoring the hold man, Peter pulled the rock salt from his belt. He scooped a handful, squeezing it tight in his fist. He'd seen how powerful the salt could be, and wanted to use as little as possible. Jerry Fisher only deserved as much.

Fisher's disfigured form clambered to its feet.

You're desperate, Phobos . . . What happens to you when you don't have a body, huh? Like a fish out of water? Let's find out.

Peter flung a handful of salt, smacking the ruined neck. It sizzled on impact.

Peter stepped back as the body thumped to the floor and shook as if electrocuted. Its limbs kicked about in a frenzy before finally falling still.

Peter's breathing sounded loud in the sudden silence. A quiet sizzling came from Jerry's body, like meat on a frying pan. Then smoke drifted from the corpse.

"Stay dead, you rotten bastard . . . Just stay dead."

Henry approached, his face gaunt. Sweat beaded his face, a glossy sheen coating his eyes. He needed medical attention. And soon.

"How did he do that?" Henry asked. "Jerry's head was caved in."

"Desperation. Panic."

Peter hated to admit it, but for the briefest moment, he related to the monster.

He cleared his throat. "Cramming into those useless corpses is a last resort to get at us. He knows damn well the bodies aren't sustainable, he's just using them as weapons. He's frightened."

"In that case there's five more corpses he's going to use, Peter."

Peter counted. Walter still lay out in the snow, then came Andrew, Jamie, Paul, and . . . Donald. Each a despicable slop of rot, but in Phobos' desperation, he'd use up what energy he had left to do the job.

"How much salt we got left?" Henry asked.

"Enough. I wasted a handful throwing blind just there. Hit clothes, hit the floor . . . Need to get a clear shot at the flesh. But getting close is dangerous. Headless or not, that fucker's got use of hands, legs, all sorts. We need a trap or something."

Henry arched an eyebrow. "A trap, sure . . . Or we use that goddamn shotgun and prepare some salt shells."

Peter couldn't help but grin. "That'd work? You know how?"

"It'd work," Henry said. "But not like in the movies. Rock salt packed in shells wouldn't even pierce skin, but we don't need it to, do we? We just need it to reach him from a distance, and the spread of a shotgun guarantees a hit."

"You're a genius, Randolph."

"Damn straight. Now go get that shotgun, I want to show you something."

At the gun rack, Peter rattled the lock. Too thick to pull free. With a deep breath, he rammed his elbow into the door. A sharp crack rang out as the wood split. He smashed the door again, this time creating a jagged hole the size of a tennis ball. Reaching in, he ripped the wood free, pulling away chunks. With a sufficient hole, Peter removed the shotgun and peered inside. A worn cardboard case of shells sat on the cabinet floor and Peter took them, too, before returning to Henry.

"Got it."

Henry lifted a book with his free hand, the other still pressing the shirt to his wound. "Look here. See the sun and moon? The layout depicts time. The ink splotch fading below? I think without a body, Phobos is going to disappear. It's only a matter of time."

Like a fish out of water, Peter thought again, a swell of hope jabbing his chest. "What do we do now? How do we prepare these shells?"

"Find me something to patch them with, search the dresser by the window."

Peter routed inside the top drawer, tossing aside a notepad, pencils, some magazines, and . . .

"Duct tape?"

"Perfect, bring it here."

Peter handed the roll to Henry, hoping there was enough left for the job. "Rip a piece of that shirt and stick it to your neck, too. Can't keep it held there forever."

A smile lifted the corner of Henry's mouth. "Shit we got no alcohol lying around, huh? Could've come in handy."

"Disinfectant, right."

"Yeah, that, too."

"It hurts bad, huh?" Peter asked. "You've lost a lot of color."

Henry tried ripping the shirt but only stretched the material. He handed it to Peter without a word. Peter ripped the cleanest section free by working his fingers into the neck hole. He wiped Henry's neck clean with the rest of the shirt before taping the patch in place. Job done, Henry pointed to the box of shells.

"Empty them, would you?"

Peter upturned the carton on the table and the shells rolled about. He counted eight in total, each with a red casting and gold-plated bottom.

Henry lifted one to study. "Standard twelve-gauge shot. Common on farms. My uncle had 'em all over the place."

The old man went to the fireplace and removed a table leg. "This'll do."

He worked the splintered end into the top of the shell vigorously. As he did, Peter watched the wound on the old man's neck. The shirt had soaked through already, black with blood. The tape seemed to hold for now, but Peter wondered for how long.

"Here we go. Look." Henry shook out pellets into the palm of his shaking hand. "Twenty-odd balls. It's buckshot. Birdshot would have about seventy. Sometimes you'll even find a single slug in here, for use on anything larger than a deer. We just need the shell, anyway. I'll empty 'em and you fill with the salt, okay?"

"Okay."

"We tape the top with that duct tape and pray it holds. Let's see the gun."

Peter passed the weapon and Henry rotated it in his hands while squinting. "Standard Remington. Holds four shells. Means you'll have to reload at least once to get all six, if we're right about the body count. But overall, not a bad weapon to be left with in a life-or-death situation."

"Why don't you—"

Henry shook his head. "Don't even ask, you're smarter than that. Look at how bad I'm shaking . . . Besides, it's a shotgun, it sprays. You don't need to be one hundred percent accurate. Don't be afraid." He gave Peter a look. "You've never shot a shotgun before, have you?"

"I've never shot any kind of gun before."

"Nothing to worry about. You see right here? Yeah. That's where the shells are inserted. You pump this here . . . To put one in the barrel. I don't think I need to explain to you what the trigger is for. Get it good and tight against your armpit to avoid kickback. That's about it. Not rocket science."

Henry gave a nervous chuckle.

"What?" Peter asked.

"It's just funny, isn't it? An ancient god, all powerful, all feared, but that was eons ago . . . We've moved on since, the whole world . . . Now two alcoholics with a shotgun full of salt are going to take it down. The times, Peter, they've changed."

"And that's what this ancient bastard never counted on. God or not, put a shotgun in its face and the fuck's gonna run . . . How'd you know so much about guns?"

"Only shotguns, actually. My uncle Richard had a farm deep down in York County. Used to spend whole summers there when I was about nine or ten. A man's man, you know the type. Used to say that the world was getting soft, that's how he worded it. *Getting soft.* Said we were forgetting how to fend for ourselves and relying too much on corporate *bigheads* to hand-feed us. Looked me right in the eye and said he'd be damned if his own blood was going to turn out the same. Each hunting season, we'd go get us some bucks and he'd explain all about shooting, all about tracking . . . I never forgot a word. My own father wasn't much use. Richard was my mother's brother, the only male role model, really, now that I think about it . . ."

The old man's eyes grew distant as he got washed away in his own memories.

"Henry," Peter said. "You all right?"

"Fine . . . Fine . . . It's just funny, isn't it? How things can go so wrong. So different. I'm just thinking . . . How does it get so bad? I never wanted to be like this, you know? I never had an interest in drinking when I was a teenager like so many of my friends seemed to. I was focused. I had drive. I just don't know where I slipped up . . . How I became so . . . Well, this."

I'm well aware, Peter thought. *Well aware.*

Peter himself never drank until touring with the band. And even then, it wasn't much. The odd complimentary bottle from the venue, left backstage at a gig, that sort of thing. Then a complimentary bottle of wine gradually became a complimentary case of beer. Soon enough, a shot of whiskey would chase that, and before Peter knew it, the whiskey got chased with something else. In no time at all, it seemed, Peter woke a decade later in a puddle of his own mess.

"You're a good man, Henry," he said. "I got to know a guy who had my back even if it meant putting himself in danger. You looked out for me. That's more than anyone else I know would be willing to do. Even so called *friends* I've known for my whole life. I didn't see an alcoholic."

Henry's lip quivered. "You're gonna get through this, Peter."

"*We're* going to. I won't let you give up hope."

"I'm not giving up hope . . . I'm just a realist, something I've always been. Peter, I was *useful* for once in my miserable piece of shit life." Henry chuckled but his eyes held steady. "My actions *meant* something. I didn't run and try to hide in the bottom of a bottle, and not just because I couldn't, because I *didn't want to*. Something more important called me. I needed to help you get through this."

Peter's throat hurt. His eyes stung, and not because of the smoke filled room. "I don't know what to say."

"Say nothing. Just do it. Face that bastard down and send him packin' with his tail between his legs. I just hope when it's time for me to go that I don't end up there. In that place."

"You think it's Hell?"

"I believe it's something very close, at least. Some unspeakable place full of monsters and daemons . . . I want to end up with my Lauren. And if there is a God, a good one, I mean, then I believe that's where I'll go. I have to."

Peter taped the last shell and placed it with the others. They were much lighter now that they'd been emptied of their pellets, but he trusted Henry when the old man said they'd do damage.

Smoky air drifted from Peter's lips. He wondered how much time they'd have before the place went up. Then another idea came. Henry smiled to him as if reading his mind.

Peter removed an invisible carton of cigarettes from his jeans pocket and presented them to Henry. Taking one, the old man snorted a laugh and made a clicking sound with his tongue, making the noise of a lighter. He breathed deeply before exhaling smoky air.

"Smoke 'em if you've got 'em, right?"

"Right." Peter faked lighting his own invisible cigarette. "Really hits the spot, doesn't it?"

"Sure does."

They stayed that way for a moment, the tension lifting slightly. Peter wanted to stay that way for as long as possible and not allow the impending sense of doom to overtake him. Every time he thought of what they were about to do, his stomach lurched. But for now, the brief moment with his friend made him smile.

"This is just like what I used to do," Henry said. "When I worked. I'd procrastinate and have smoke after smoke before finally getting the job started. Always." He took another drag on the invisible butt and grinned. "But you know what? I'd always get the job done once I finally did manage to start. And well, too, I might add."

"I hope this one won't be any different."

"Me, too."

Henry passed the shotgun to Peter. He tapped the shirt on his neck and winced. The duct tape had come undone at one end, saturated in blood and no longer sticking. He pressed it back into place and waited for Peter to load the gun.

Pumping the shotgun, Peter placed the four remaining shells full of rock salt into his jeans pocket and nodded. The sharp smell of smoke tickled his nose and made his eyes water.

"We should head outside. I think the kitchen's caught, for sure. Whole place might go up any second now. When that happens, the nearest town's bound to send some rescue chopper or something to investigate. *Our* ticket out of here."

"Sure." Henry never looked him in the eye as he spoke, and Peter knew the old man had accepted his fate here in the Dawson farmhouse. He'd made his peace with the fact that he'd never get out alive. But Peter hadn't.

"Let's move."

A thump came from within the room. Peter pulled the shotgun tight against his shoulder and aimed.

"Go behind me, Henry."

Keeping the gun raised, Peter sidestepped the broken door, kicking shards from his path. He chanced a glance into the hallway and saw the staircase and far wall lit in a dancing orange glow. He'd been right; the kitchen now blazed.

The carpet covering Donald's body rustled. Peter took aim and waited, his heart hammering his ribcage. The idea of Phobos, now desperate, wriggling into the destroyed corpse of their dead friend made him want to scream. Donald might not have much of a head anymore, but he had big hands for scratching and big muscles for grabbing. The corpse still had to be warm, maybe they'd get lucky and Rigor mortis would—

Peter's thoughts cut as the makeshift cover on Donald's body lifted. It looked like a worm made of carpet, sitting up in a backwards capital L. With a shout, Peter pulled the trigger.

Please don't jam . . .

The shotgun kicked as the bang crashed throughout the farmhouse. Donald's body dropped, the carpet flaked with holes. Wisps of smoke rose from the tiny tears and the sound of sizzling meat followed.

Shaking his head, Peter thanked Henry for covering their friend's body. He didn't want to see another corpse move, especially not Donald.

The prayer only lasted a second, however, as Paul's corpse spasmed.

The orderly beneath the curtain jerked and twisted, his limbs stretched straight and long. His legs drummed the hardwood. Pumping the shotgun, Peter pulled the trigger a second time.

Paul's body flopped still. The salt ripped through the carpet as easy as led through paper. The fresh holes looked as if worms had burrowed. Smoke trailed away once again, and the fizzing sound added to the noise coming from Donald's corpse.

The smell of cooking flesh ghosted beneath the smoke. Wiping his eyes, Peter nodded towards the hallway and pumped another shell into the barrel of the shotgun.

"Come on, we don't have much time left. We'll meet Walter before he gets in here."

In the hallway, the scorching heat stroked Peter's bare skin. He thought of Jamie and Shelly's bodies down in the basement, ruined, sure, but if Phobos was desperate . . .

"You think he'd take Shelly or Jamie?"

"I don't know if he could."

"He might. *Don't know* isn't going to cut it here, we can't allow it. I think he'll go for Walter or Andrew first. Let's start with them."

A figure sloshed through the snow from the far side of the

yard. Pointing the barrel, Peter watched the corpse of Walter Cartwright come closer and closer. Walter's innards slopped away from his sliced open stomach, like saliva dripping from the jaw of a pit bull. Their old friend smiled, his crooked glasses still glued to his face as if by magic. Fat, gray skin flapped as he staggered forward.

"*You worthless pieces of shit!*" Phobos roared. His voice sounded like a muddy pipe. "*How dare you! I am Phobos and you will fear me! You will! I'll pick your bones from my teeth by the time this is through. Save yourself the trouble and walk back into that kitchen to choke . . . Do it in my name. I demand it.*"

The dead body of Walter Cartwright climbed the porch steps, but never made it to the door. For the third time, Peter squeezed the trigger and dropped a former friend.

Walter's head bucked, his legs struggling to keep him upright. His arms cartwheeled, trying to maintain balance. His right foot clomped onto the porch, splashing a puddle of his own juices and innards. When his head fell back into place, it bouncing on the stalk of his thick neck. Peter saw he'd made a direct hit with the salt. Holes peppered their fallen friend's face.

Phobos screamed as the tiny openings began to sizzle and smoke. His hands slapped at his face, pulling the skin. He pinched the cuts with one hand as the other wriggled inside, trying to get to the embedded salt grains. Then he peeled his hands away, pulling strings of melting flesh like mozzarella cheese. Snot-like, red threads stuck to his fingers, and he frantically flung them away, wailing in agony. Thin tendrils of smoke trailed above his head and out into the night sky. The flesh around his eyes melted down his peppered cheeks, leaving the eyeballs bare and exposed.

Peter pumped another shell into the barrel of the shotgun.

"Wait, Peter! You don't need to waste another one, he's going down."

"*Yes!*" Walter hissed. "*Save all the salt you need, boy. All the salt within the oceans of the world if that's what it takes . . . But know this . . .*" Phobos pointed a gore soaked finger at Peter's face. "*It will never be enough.*"

Walter's body reeled back and crashed down the porch steps

before landing face down in the snow. He spasmed as the salt burned through to the bone, then he lay still.

Peter looked to Henry and shook his head slowly. He felt like getting sick. "Andrew's next... Jesus I wish I didn't have to do any of this."

"They're already dead, don't forget that. If anything, you're doing them a favor. You think Walter would want to be possessed by that . . . That *thing*?" He said the word as if it left a bad taste in his mouth. "Donald, too? Don would have thanked you for days knowing you put him down. He died honorably, and that son-of-a-bitch Phobos desecrated his remains. *You* set it right. And that's what you're going to keep on doing now, okay? You're going to keep doing it because you have to. You *need* to."

Peter fell silent a moment. He turned the shotgun over in his hands, admiring how the light glistened off the barrel. "How's your neck?" He asked.

For a second, Henry didn't answer. By the glazed look in his eyes, and by his labored breathing, Peter knew that the pain had to bad. He wondered how much time they had left. A chopper ride out of here couldn't take more than twenty minutes to the nearest hospital. Surely Henry could hold on for that long. Couldn't he?

Finally, Henry spoke. "I'm not going to lie, Peter. It's bad. I'm shaking, and there's colored spots doing a flamenco dance across my eyes . . . Cut's stinging, too. Feels like it's infected."

"Well just hold on just a little longer, man. We'll take care of Andrew."

A hair-curling laugh ripped through the darkness. It carried on the wind and echoed throughout the woodlands. Then the night fell silent again.

Peter kept his voice down and pointed to where Andrew's body lay. He squeezed the shotgun in his hands, reassuring himself with the weight. "Look out there."

Peter shivered at the change in temperature as he stepped along the porch. A pillar of frosted breath poured from his lips and he took the steps down into the snow, making sure to avoid Walter's fallen body.

The poor fuck . . .

A single trench left by Walter cut through the otherwise perfect blanket of snow. Peter avoided it like a contagious cancer. He didn't want to step anywhere near where that creature had. Instead, he began cutting his own path across the yard, his bootheels crunching the white powder.

Henry called from the porch. "Hey! I can't go out there . . . I think I'd pass out. I just can't do it."

"That's all right. Wait there." Peter continued forward, his eyes trained on the thing lifting itself at the bottom of the yard. A monstrosity that used to go by the name Andrew.

Using Walter's teeth, Phobos had stripped the flesh away from the orderly's bones. The skeleton now sitting in the snow had no lips, its teeth appearing too large and all too exposed. Eyeballs rolled about in their raw sockets, lacquered in a crimson goop. A slab of flesh still capped Andrew's red hair to the top of the otherwise bare skull.

The skeleton chattered its teeth, and stood.

"*More salt for me, Peter Laughlin? More salt?*"

Using Walter, Phobos had torn away chunks of Andrew's throat, leaving the voice strangled and tight. Ribbons of meat lay in rags around the orderly's chest, leaving the bare Adam's apple to bob around as he spoke. "*Do what you will, Peter. It won't be enough. It will never be enough.*"

The skeleton of Andrew crashed back into the snow as Peter pulled the trigger, the skull spraying away in a shower of shattered bone. Brain matter painted the snow with flecks of red. Rooks cried out in the forest beyond the yard, taking flight into the night sky and seeking a quieter place to rest. Peter envied them.

"Peter!" Henry called from the porch. "Get back here, hurry."

As Peter slogged for the house, Henry held one of the porch's beams for support. He looked as pale, his skin waxy and shriveled. "He's stalling you. Get back here and take care of the other two, hurry."

"Stalling me?"

Peter climbed the porch while loading the final four shells into the shotgun. His hands shook from the cold and the adrenaline but he managed to complete the task.

"Yes. Look at this cut . . . You know what I'm talking about. That cat's attack was calculated. I'm a dead man walking and all he's trying to do is stall you until I'm gone because then he has a usable body to host."

Peter pumped the gun. "Well then let's get those two before he gets the chance and get you to a hospital, right?"

Henry grabbed his arm. "Don't be a fool, we run for it, now! If Phobos hosts in either one of those two downstairs he'll burn up by the time anyone responds to the fire. He'll be without a body and he'll disappear. Let's *go*."

"And what if he doesn't, Henry? What if he finds a way to avoid burning and waits until someone gets up here? Once anyone breaks that salt barrier, they're his. We can't allow any room for doubt. We can't let this thing out into the world. I need to destroy those bodies completely, Henry, I do."

"Peter . . ."

Peter pushed his way into the hallway and made for the dining-room door, smoke curling and trickling from around its frame.

Once I finished with these two things in the cellar, I'm keeping you lucid, Henry . . . Then we'll get out of here together. That sonofabitch isn't taking you.

"Peter! Don't be a fool!"

Peter stopped and turned, the fire roaring from beyond the dining-room door. "If we run right now you'll collapse in the woods. *You won't make it, Henry.* Now I'm dropping those two downstairs before the fire gets too much and then we're getting out of here and that's final. That's all there is to say on this."

Peter pushed open the dining room door and stepped inside the burning room.

CHAPTER EIGHTEEN

A fat gray cloud had replaced the dining room. Thick smoke wafted over Peter, enclosing him in an impenetrable blanket. He grimaced and covered his mouth with his free arm but the smoke still got through, stinging his eyes. Warm tears slid down his cheeks.

He wheezed. "*Oh sweet fucking Jesus . . .*"

Taking a deep breath, he pushed into the room, the plump smoke curling around him. The door to the hallway disappeared. Peter's world went from black to gray, black to gray as he blinked away the stream of tears. On his right, towards the kitchen swing door, the smoke pulsed an orange-red from the fire, and holding his breath, he darted in that direction.

His shin clipped one of the overturned armchairs and sharp pain zapped up his leg. The wound there throbbed. Peter winced and resisted the urge to take an agonizing breath. Feeling with the shotgun, he prodded into the smoke, seeking the kitchen door. The barrel smacked a wall, starling him. He almost pulled the trigger out of fright but managed to keep calm. He needed oxygen. He needed to take a breath. A headache pulsed behind his irritated eyes.

Then he found the door. Using his shoulder, Peter slammed it open and fell inside the scorching hot room.

He wanted to scream out, the heat too intense, but instead he sunk his teeth into his forearm and rushed for the stairway beneath the sink. There had to be less smoke down there, just had to. Either way, he needed to take a breath soon, regardless. He felt lightheaded.

Rushing through the kitchen, the fire roared from out of sight, lost in the black void of smoke. A sound filled his ears like constant thunder. His skin tightened and stung from the heat, cooking. Peter prodded the shotgun at leg height, manically searching for the hole beneath the sink that led to the cellar.

Where is the goddamn stairs, please! I need to get home . . . I need to get home and see my—

The shotgun barrel slipped inside the open cupboard. Saying a silent thank you, Peter got on all fours and scrambled down the stairwell, heading for the cellar.

The temperature instantly dropped, not by much, but enough. At the bottom of the stairs, Peter chanced a breath. His lungs stung but at least the air here contained a little oxygen. Wiping the sweat from his brow, he fell towards the cellar door. Then he stepped in something.

He stepped in Shelly Matthews.

The liquefied blob of flesh quivered like a fried egg beneath his heel. One eye blinked within the mess and stared back at him. Then a sloppy hand gripped his ankle. Peter's stomach lurched. He shouted and lifted his leg, pulling away from the weak grip before pointing the shotgun down. He pulled the trigger.

The flash lit the room for a split second. Peter's hearing disappeared instantly, replaced by a sharp ringing that sent him off balance. Slipping on Shelly Matthew's remains, Peter crashed back onto the steps, winding himself. What little oxygen he had left in his lungs blew out, substituted by choking smoke. Blind spots danced across his vision. His back throbbed from the fall.

"Oh, you fucking idiot," he wheezed. "Get the hell up . . ."

Grunting, Peter used the shotgun to help him stand and pulled himself to his feet. He coughed and gasped, trying to catch his breath. Panic began to set in at the idea of passing out.

Relax, he told himself. *Come on, let your muscles loosen up and suck some goddamn oxygen . . .*

Then something came through the smoke as fast as a freight train, slamming him in the chest and sending him crashing to the lower stair. A loud crack of wood rang out and the little breath left in Peter's lungs rushed out in a painful whistle. An unbearable pressure pushed into his chest, constricting his breathing. By the smell alone, Peter knew that the ruined remains of Jamie Peters bore down on him.

"*Get . . . off . . .*"

"Why, Peter Laughlin," Phobos said using Jamie's mouth. He pushed his brow into Peters and smiled. An overwhelming stench drifted from Jamie's shredded neck, brown and rank like rancid meat. "Why would I go and do that? You've got such a beautiful body for me, and with so much *use* left. Not that *you'll* do anything useful with it. Leaving you with it would be a waste. I won't be greedy this time. No, I'll take it slow and gentle . . . Slide inside of you as if you were a virgin on their first night of romance. Don't worry, I'll take it easy . . ."

Peter mouthed the words *get fucked*, but his voice refused to work. The weight on his chest increased. His vision began to disappear as his eyes fluttered closed. He tried to force them open but they felt made of lead. They continued to shut.

Peter's world went dark, and the roar of the fire in the kitchen became less alarming and increasingly soothing. Something cold slithered around his throat, and in the back of his mind, Peter knew that it was Jamie's dead hands, but he didn't mind. The time had come to sleep.

Someone shouted from somewhere very far away. Peter wished they'd shut up. It sounded like an argument, somewhere down the street outside of his apartment window. Probably junkies. He wished they'd stop. He needed to drift away . . .

"—*Off him!*"

Stinging air rushed inside his lungs as Peter's world exploded back into view. He bolted upright, his neck aching and his vision pulsing. The deformed corpse of Jamie Peters clutched at its face, dark locks of sweaty hair flying in every direction. Goop oozed from between trembling fingers as the body collapsed in the corner and spasmed.

Peter arched his head and saw Henry standing halfway up the staircase, the bag of rock salt clutched in his right hand. His other hand pressed his neck, covering the mess of shirt. He looked colorless, drained of energy. Behind him, the kitchen blazed like the depths of hell, making him a silhouette.

Peter strained to speak, the unclean air leaving him sick. "We need to get out of here," he said. "The whole place is going up."

Peter wobbled up the steps, using the shotgun as a cane.

Henry coughed. "Stop being an idiot, Peter. Leave me down here. Let me burn up. He'll get no use out of me. I'll make sure of it."

"Shut up and move, old man."

Peter grabbed Henry by the arm and pulled him behind. Henry resisted at first but Peter guessed survival instinct kicked in because then Henry kept pace.

Good. You've played the hero already, Henry. Let's get you out of here.

Peter's breath streamed away in thick clouds of smoke. The air stank of charred wood. Peter tightened his grip on Henry's sleeve.

"Jesus," Peter shouted back, the smoke gagging him. "I can't see a thing . . ."

Peter's hand tore free of Henry as the old man tripped on a step and went over, falling flat on his stomach.

Peter's stomach pulled tight as he ducked and searched for the old man. "Henry, are you all right? Speak to me."

The old man raised his head, hardly visible in the dense gray, and relief washed through Peter. Henry nodded and pushed himself to his feet. He smiled sheepishly.

"Sorry . . ."

Coughing, Peter flapped his hand for Henry to take and once the old man had a hold, he climbed the last steps of the staircase.

"We're going to have to make a break for it," Peter said, his voice muffled in his forearm. "Through the kitchen, so just follow my lead, okay? Don't slow, not even for a second. And take a damn deep breath right now."

Without another word, Peter leaped from the hole in the cupboard and emerged into the inferno.

Fire danced up the walls and licked the ceiling, charring it black. It bellied and burst, reaching for him. The sickening smell of singed hair filled his nose and Peter realized it came from him. Then something hissing from within the wall of flames. A memory sprung to Peter's mind.

The propane canisters Paul had used . . .

Terror settled inside Peter as he scrambled to the left, working from memory to find the swing door.

We're gonna burn up . . .

Peter bolted without thought, his legs tripping over themselves. The fire rumbled, a low guttural sound, screaming at him to stay.

The shotgun bobbed against his chest as Peter dashed forward, hoping he connected with a door and not a wall. The swing door smashed open and Peter fell out into the dining room. The smoke was thicker than ever, if he wanted to breathe, he'd have to get out now. Peter shot through the room, smacking his shin for a second time on the fallen armchair. His wound howled. For a moment, he almost his lost balance and but managed to shuffle away in an awkward hop. Hitting the breakfast table, he pulled it from the doorway and stumbled out into the hall. The alarm still screamed.

Peter raced for the front door, his boots smacking the floorboards. Taking the porch in one leap, he crashed in the snow and sucked cold, fresh air into his burning lungs. The icy cold tightened his too-hot flesh as he rolled about, whimpering with joy. He knew that somewhere to his left lay the fallen corpse of Walter Cartwright, but right now that didn't seem to matter. All that mattered now was that he was outside, and safe.

The kitchen at the other side of the farmhouse crackled and screamed as it went up in flames. Embers danced up over the rooftop and out into the night sky. The mostly wooden house would be engulfed in a matter of minutes.

"Henry . . ."

Panic settled in as Peter sat up and looked to the house. An explosion erupted from the back and he ducked, squeezing his eyes shut.

The first propane tank, he thought.

A fireball rose like an orange fist into the night and dispersed in a cloud of embers.

"Henry!"

Peter's voice echoed throughout the farmyard, the only response coming from the fire as it gurgling away. Peter stood and eyed the front door, willing Henry to appear.

Come on, come on . . .

How could he be so stupid? How could he have left the old man behind? He needed to go back inside.

Peter stumbled towards the porch steps but froze as he reached them. Henry Randolph stood at the front door, flames dancing behind him like the gateway to hell. Shadows danced across his waxy complexion, his stance off to one side. That sheepish smile still played on his face.

Peter shook his head and sniffled. "I was going to go back and get you. I thought you were behind me . . ."

Looking into Henry's eyes, fear slithered up Peter's spine. He'd seen that look before, from when Walter stood at the window, gazing in on them like they were toys in a gift shop. Henry's eyes were lifeless. Henry's eyes were dead.

Pumping the shotgun, Peter took a step back. "Don't you fucking move, you sonofabitch."

The shotgun trembled in his hands. The cold felt stronger now, bitter and sharp. Snow crunched beneath his feet as he retreated.

"Peter," Henry replied, clicking his tongue in a *tisk-tisk* fashion. "Please don't point that thing at me."

Henry stepped onto the porch and Peter jabbed the shotgun at him. "I said don't fucking move!"

When had it happened? Had Henry choked inside while Peter fled? The old man said he had a dodgy heart . . . How could Peter have let him out of his sight?

"Come, now," Henry said. "Help will be here soon. The fire should signal the furthest town. Anybody with a heart would call for help, right? Soon we can get out of here and take me to a hospital. Make me *aaaaall* better."

"Stop it."

"We can have a cigarette when all this is done, eh? Go visit that little lady friend of yours and set things straight. Wouldn't that be sweet? See your child born, perhaps even make a godparent out of me, if you would be so kind. And to heck with it, have a tequila or a beer to celebrate. Or both. What's to lose? We're both burdens, anyhow."

"Henry Randolph was a brave man. An honest, good man."

Peter stepped towards his friend's walking corpse. His hands had stopped shaking. All fear had dissolved, replaced with nothing but determination and pure, seething anger. "You underestimated us. Maybe a long, long time ago people dropped to their knees for you and you might have had all the power in the world, but what are you now, huh? What are you now besides *irrelevant*? You're *nothing*."

Phobos snarled, contorting Henry's features in a way they'd never moved before.

Peter ignored the taunt. "Great god or not, that doesn't matter now. These days even a loser with a shotgun full of salt can waste you." Peter aimed for Henry's head and swallowed the lump in his throat. "You underestimated a man who's got nothing to lose."

The shot boomed through the farmyard. Henry's body went over, crashing to the porch, peppered with holes. Tendrils of smoke lulled away from the sizzling body and Peter turned, unable to watch. Tears welled in his eyes. He blinked them away and took a deep, unsteady breath. In the back of his mind, he knew Phobos still lurked, flying through the night, desperately seeking another body to host before time ran out and he dissolved into nothingness.

Peter sniffled, wiping his running nose on his arm. He dropped the shotgun and fell to his knees, an involuntary scream forcing its way up from the depths of his stomach. His throat ripped as he roared into the night. "You see this, you cocksucker? I'm useful! I'm worth something! I'm *somebody*! You're *nothing*! Nobody needs you! I'm not afraid of you! I have people waiting at home for me who care about me . . . I have people who care . . ." Peter's chest ached. He rubbed at his nose, wiping away cold liquid. His shoulders hitched. People *cared* about him. People *loved* him. If he could just get back home to Beth and *talk* to her, he stood a chance of having a family . . . An actual *family*. No matter how minuscule a chance that might actually be.

A light lit up over the treetops like a distant star. The hum of an engine cut through the roar of the fire. Peter watched in shock as a helicopter drifted closer, its blades chopping the air.

He fell to his knees and cradled his face. "Thank you . . . *Thank you*."

He cried for Henry. He cried for Donald and Walter. He cried for all the others who lost their lives because of Jerry Fisher and Harris Dawson. But mostly, he cried for himself. Not out of sadness. Out of joy. He was *alive*.

He had a life to start, one with a chance.

Peter's vision blurred from the tears, multiplying the helicopter. He wiped his eyes but the choppers stayed. Three of them.

Cold air rushed over Peter's skin as the choppers lowered into the bottom of the yard, kicking up snow in all directions. Peter covered his face and breathed through his mouth, the loud blades wheezing down in an ear-busting screech. Trees bent, flailing in the sharp gusts. Then the rotor-blades fell still, the engines still jittering.

The side doors on all three choppers flew open and ten men hoped into the snow, one of them yelling orders, his voice muffled behind his headgear.

. . . Are they wearing riot uniforms?

Flashlights clicked on and blinded him. Peter squinted and craned his neck to see beyond the glare, scanning the cockpits of the three choppers. His heart skipped a beat as he found exactly what he hoped he would not: A man in his mid to late sixties sitting in the leftmost helicopter, wearing a black winter jacket and a woolen hat.

". . . Harris Dawson."

The group of men jogged towards the house, and Peter recoiled as he saw their flashlights mounted to assault rifles. A badge adorned each of their chests. A logo of some sort.

Peter recalled Jerry Fisher's story of how Dawson's work got funded. How Dawson Rehabilitation was nothing but a cover for the man's true research. Whoever funded it must have an awful lot of money. Perhaps enough to hire a small army to keep everything under wraps and leave no evidence . . .

One of the men stepped forward, flanked by two others.

"In position," he shouted. "Go!"

The seven remaining men shot towards the house, their rifles raised. The man in front of Peter lowered his gun, his face obscured by his visor. Peter could hear someone speak via a headphone set inside of the helmet. The man nodded then turned his attention back to Peter. "Sir, Mr. Laughlin, you need to come with us."

Peter wasn't afraid. He'd had enough of that already. "Where?"

The man listened to his head-piece once more before nodding. "That information is classified, Mr. Laughlin."

"Who are you people? Why doesn't Dawson come down here himself and see the mess he's made? See the *lives* his research has cost? Hell, I should just kill one of you and let Phobos take your body, let you all see the monster he's unleashed into this world! Do you even know what's going on here?"

At that, the two flanking soldiers raised their rifles. Peter walked towards one, pressing the cold steel of the barrel to his chest. Sharp pressure sunk from the tip into his ribcage. He pressed harder and looked the soldier in the face. "Go on. Do it. You'll be unleashing a monster. You know that. Don't intimidate me with your big guns, little man. Lower it and get on with whatever it is that asshole is paying you to do."

Peter turned his attention to Harris Dawson in the chopper and flipped him the finger. Even at this distance, Peter could see a smirk spread across the bastard's face.

You find this amusing, you sick fuck?

"Fine," Peter said. "I'll go with you. Not like I have a whole lot of other options. Lead the way."

"Subject is on route to Chopper A," the first soldier said into his headset. "Stand by." He turned back to Peter. "Come with me."

Peter followed the man back to the helicopter. Halfway across the yard, he chanced a glance back at the farmhouse and watched as the dining-room collapsed. Fat flames lapped at the night sky, each one reaching higher than the last.

Good riddance to it. Let it burn. Let it all burn. The books. The bodies. Turn them to ash and let them be forgotten.

A smile spread across Peter's face as he trudged on. Back home, his grandmother waited. Beth waited. His child waited. Whatever these people planned to do with him, he did not know. But neither did he care.

He'd lived enough of his life in fear.

Things were going to happen, good things, bad things, and he had no control. All he could do was walk forward with his head held high and his destination set, for better or for worse. If these men wanted to kill him, then that's what they would do. If that happened, Peter wouldn't know either way. They'd probably take him out with a silenced pistol in the back of the head on the chopper ride. He wouldn't know, either way. And that didn't scare him.

The soldier opened the helicopter side-door and waved Peter onboard. Peter climbed in without a word, taking a seat and buckling his belt. Two of the men climbed in beside him and sat with their guns across their laps. Peter returned to his thoughts.

Those men didn't scare him.

If they let him go home, well then he'd spend what few days his grandmother had left with her, building up a bank of memories. Memories he'd cherish and keep until the end of *his* days, no matter how many were left. He'd make a visit to Beth. If she wanted to see him.

Even if she didn't, all he could do was offer his support for their child and make sure she knew he'd be there. He'd always be there. She deserved the best, and Peter would try his hardest to be that for her. His best. After all, for the first time he could remember, he was clean.

There was a chance he could see his child. That chance, no matter how small, was the greatest thought of all. It made his heart jump into the back of his throat. It made his stomach quiver. A kid was on the way.

A grandmother, a possible partner, and a child . . . That was more than enough reason to keep going. Far more than he thought he'd ever deserve or get. And because of that, he kept his head high as the engine picked up in volume.

The pilot called back. "Takeoff in five."

For the first time in years, Peter's fingers itched to play the guitar. Songs brewed inside him again, that old familiar feeling making his whole being sing with excitement. A visit from the Muse, like Santa Claus... The possibility of creation. Peter welcomed the longtime friend with open arms. Music needed to be made. So much music.

Perhaps enough to start a career again. A comeback album. Solo record. To hell with everyone else. He'd go it alone. He'd simply do whatever it was that he could. That was enough. Because most importantly, he was going to live.

And all the fear in the world wasn't going to stop him.

ACKNOWLEDGMENTS

Thanks to: Conor McMahon, Bob Ford, Tristan Thorne, Matt Worthington, Erin Sweet-Al Mehairi, Patrick Lacey, David Murphy, Russell Coy, Kealan Patrick Burke, Elizabeth Jenike, Eric Beebe, John Urbancik, Os Andres, Kevin Liffey, Cooper Gordon, and Ivan Byrne.

POST MORTEM PRESS
www.postmortem-press.com

About Post Mortem Press

Since its inception in 2010, Post Mortem Press has published over 100 titles in the genres of dark fiction, suspense/mystery, horror, and dark fantasy. The goal is to provide a showcase for talented authors, affording exposure and opportunity to "get noticed" by the mainstream publishing community. Post Mortem Press has quickly become a powerful voice in the small genre press community. The result has been five years of steady growth and successful endeavors that have garnered attention from all across the publishing world.

Made in the USA
Lexington, KY
05 April 2018